River of Fire

BETTIE WILSON STORY

Chariot Books

Special appreciation goes to the Historical Library of the Mobile Public Library, Mobile, Alabama, who provided most of the research materials for this story.

RIVER OF FIRE

First printing, November, 1978
Second printing, February, 1979

Published by David C. Cook Publishing Co., Elgin, IL 60120
Edited by Janet Hoover Thoma

Designed by Kurt Dietsch
Cover illustration by Dennis Bellile
Inside illustrations by Larry Taylor

Printed in the United States of America
Library of Congress Catalog Number: 78-68434
ISBN: 0-89191-170-7

No cabins. No plowed fields. No trails in the undergrowth. Malinda is alone in the Alabama wilderness. . . .

Until Jasmine, a runaway slave girl, finds her. Forced together to survive, they hide in the dark swamplands by day and canoe the unknown waters of the Tombigbee River by night . . . two fugitives searching for a path to Mobile.

Then they hear sounds of a close-by plantation, which means rescue for Malinda. But not for Jasmine, who would be returned to her master and face a cat-o'-nine-tails or even death.

Malinda must decide. Should she call out for help or continue the hazardous journey?

*In loving memory
of my grandparents –*

*Ida Mae Mathison
and William Lee Wilson
Minnie Eliza Strickland
and William Francis Monk*

Contents

1
YELLOW FEVER

MALINDA SHARP SAT ON THE EDGE of the cane chair. Hearing the mournful call of a hoot owl at the edge of the clearing, she dropped her head in weariness. Her fingers absently traced squares on the quilt that covered her mother as she watched her familiar face on the pillow. Seven days of fever had drained the rich color from mother's skin and turned it yellow. Her large, generous mouth and firm chin were lifeless.

Please, God, mama must live! Malinda prayed. *I need her. Papa needs her.* It was a litany Malinda repeated over and over.

Mary Sharp slowly opened her eyes and turned her head to look at her twelve-year-old daughter.

"How do you feel?" Malinda placed a hand on her mother's hot, dry forehead.

Mary closed her eyes briefly. "I'm fine," she whispered.

"You told papa that just before he left to repair the traps. Are you sure?"

"Yes. I want to talk, Malindy."

"Save your strength, mama. It'll keep till you're stronger."

"I'm afraid it won't get said. You're growing so, child—you're almost grown. And you haven't had a speck of schooling."

"You and papa—"

"We taught you to read, but there's much more to learn. We can't teach it all." Her breath came in short gasps.

"Please, mama, rest—"

Her mother's eyes held hers. "They have schools down in Mobile, Malindy. I've been plannin' for you to go live with your Aunt Eliza for a while—"

"I don't want to leave you and papa!"

"Promise to remember my wishes, child."

Malinda gripped her hand. "Yes, mama." She would say anything to save her mother's strength, but she would never leave them. Never!

Numb with fear, Malinda pushed back her mother's brown hair, which sparkled with gold and amber. Her mother smiled at her touch.

"Now that you have promised, please read to me. I want . . . to hear the Twenty-third Psalm."

Malinda knew it by heart, but she picked up the worn Bible from the lamp table beside the bed and turned to the psalm, forcing herself to hold the book steady.

"The Lord is my shepherd; I shall not want."

The lamplight cast eerie shadows on the cabin wall and filled Malinda with a lonely dread.

"Yea, though I walk through the valley of the shadow of death, I shall fear no evil—"

"He knew, Malindy," her mother interrupted.

"Who knew, mama?"

"The psalmist. Some folks think we find God in all the beautiful, lovely things of life. But the wilderness, Lindy—that's where we find God."

"But, mama—"

"Read, honey."

"For thou art with me. . . ."

Malinda wanted to cry out in desperation.

When she finished the psalm, her mother was in a calm sleep. Malinda picked up one of

11

the ocean stones from the lamp table and studied its designs of grey, wine, and crystal, rubbing her palm over its sea smoothness. She had treasured the stones after finding them that day on the North Carolina coast—the day Aunt Eliza had set sail for the far-off port of Mobile.

Two years later papa had moved his family overland from North Carolina to a place near the Tombigbee River. Mobile was only a few days' journey down the river, but it might as well be on the other side of the world. In five years of living in the west Alabama wilderness, they had not been able to visit Aunt Eliza.

Malinda set the ocean stone aside and laid her fingertips on her mother's cheeks. They were hot and flushed. Her fever was rising again.

There was no tea to give her; they had used it all up as the days of mama's sickness wore on. Water would never do. Mama had always said it was fatal if you had the fever, and her mother before her.

Her heart pounding, Malinda grabbed the warm herb broth she had made. "Please, mama, try to drink this," she cried.

The broth would not go down.

"Swallow, mama!"

She did not.

Malinda set the broth back on the stove, then dipped up a pan of cool spring water to bathe her mother's face and arms.

Papa! Papa! She wanted to shout and have him appear instantly in the doorway. But only the July flies filled the night with their sound.

Soon mama was delirious. She thrashed wildly about, then changed to fevered listlessness and drifted into unconsciousness.

A voice inside Malinda said, *Find papa,* but she wasn't sure that was the wisest advice. She had never gone into the forest alone at night—a rule papa demanded she obey without question. But tonight was different. It would take both of them to pull mama through this new crisis. The inside voice might be right; she needed to find him.

After bathing her mother once more with cool spring water, Malinda placed another damp cloth on her forehead. Then she closed the cabin door softly and dashed up the creek. When she did not find her father at the first trap, she followed the creek a while before deciding to strike off through the woods in search of a short cut. The image of the flushed face on the pillow drove her on to find a familiar trail.

But she did not. The forest was a strange world of its own in the dark. Soon she was entangled in dense undergrowth; twisting and turning she made her way beyond briars and swamp dogwood. Vines climbing among the smaller trees made a canopy that hid the moon. Once she thought she heard the *ha ha* sound of a Choctaw Indian's call for caution.

She pushed ahead, totally confused. In her struggle she forgot the things papa had taught her in case she lost direction. She could hardly see at all.

Then the smell of woodsmoke drew her forward, her nose searching out its location. She stared beyond the trees as she walked, and soon saw a dim fire sputtering through the branches. Was that papa? She began to run, then tripped over a log and fell head first into a clearing. The fire on the other side of the clearing was tended by several men who were shouting obscenities.

"That runawayer won't run no more!"

A colored man dangled by a rope over the fire.

Malinda curled up in revulsion and squeezed her eyes shut.

A scream split the air. It crossed the clearing in a second, bumping the tree trunks around Malinda and striking the high branches. No other sound existed, she thought. No wind, no songbirds, not even a lone coyote.

The familiar fragrance of pine smoke

She stared beyond the trees where a man dangled from a rope.

turned to stench. It filled Malinda's nostrils. Gasping for breath, she opened her eyes. The slave's feet and hair had been set on fire, enveloping him in flames.

The men laughed and cursed. "No sir! He ain't runnin' no more! I coulda took it from just him! But the fool tried to start a risin' of the field hands!"

Malinda retched.

She crawled to her feet in a daze and began to run. One of the lynchers crashed through the underbrush, clamped his arms around her, and slapped a hand over her mouth.

"You git outta here! You didn't see nothin'!"

Malinda struggled, kicking at him.

He loosened his grip. "Well, if it ain't Jeremiah Sharp's gal! What you doin' so far from home? You tell your pa we caught our nigger! You tell him, you hear?"

When she finally found her father, Malinda was sobbing, but she could not tell him what she had seen.

He held her close for a brief moment. "For sure, Malindy, you're brave—and foolish, too—to come alone. These old woods scare grown men."

If only she could feel comfort from his hug.

"There's wild animals, maybe unfriendly Creek Indians around."

Malinda wiped her eyes with a balled-up fist. "It's mama—run, papa, run!"

As they rushed home, he tried to reassure her. "It touches me deep, Malindy, that you braved the night. Don't cry now. We'll reach mama in time."

She doubled over, vomiting again. "I hate the woods! I hate them!"

When they reached home, mama's fever had risen still higher. Her skin was dry like an August creek bed, and she lay listless as death.

Papa knelt by her side, bathed her face and arms and body in cool water, and whispered his love. Malinda stood by handing him cloths, helplessly gripped in loneliness. She tormented herself with the thought that mama's worsened condition was her fault for losing her way in the forest.

She could not take her eyes away from mother's face. Papa suddenly let the cloth drop. His hunched shoulders sagged; his head dropped to his chest in despair. *Mama won't pull through,* she thought.

She reached for the Bible on the bedside table. Without opening it she whispered, "The Lord is mama's shepherd. She shall fear no evil. Is that a promise, papa?"

"Yes, honey. It's a promise."

The next day her father dug a grave by the cabin while Malinda carved on a simple wooden marker:

MARY SHARP
1804-1836

2

NO TURNING BACK

MALINDA GRIPPED THE HANDRAIL on the deck of the *Alabama Queen* as she watched slaves—no, papa called them roustabouts—load on wood for the furnace. Other slaves stacked bales of cotton that reached as high as the upper deck on each side of the steamboat. Clerks were checking goods and passengers on and off.

Most of the travelers watched the commotion on this October evening from the upper decks. But not Malinda. She wanted to be in the middle of all the excitement. It kept her from remembering that she and her father had only a few remaining minutes together.

She walked along the narrow path between the rail and the stacked cotton bales back to the huge paddle wheel. Roustabouts, dripping with sweat, stoked the furnace. Flames were visible through the doors, and the boat shuddered as if impatient to be on the move again.

But where was papa? He should be done talking to the captain by now. She ran back up the boiler deck, wistfully looking at the passengers standing above her and wishing the trip held the same gaiety for her.

The boat was huge—two-and a-half decks and a pilot house. Above it a smokestack rose on each side of the boat whistle, which had already given off a shrill blast.

She did not see papa. Instead she caught the eye of a young colored girl who was staring at her.

Malinda had never seen so many Negroes. Their nearest neighbor ten miles up the creek owned a slave, and Malinda had seen him once. She had gone with her parents sometimes to see Running Bull, their Choctaw Indian friend, and seen a few Negroes living among the Choctaws. Papa said they were runaways. The only others were several miles down the Tombigbee River on a plantation. But Malinda had never been there.

The girl still stared at Malinda. Why had

she let papa out of her sight, and why was he talking so long with the captain? As if she read her thoughts, the black girl nodded toward the main deck. Malinda looked up and saw papa coming down the steps.

She ran to him. "Papa! Where were you?"

"Just checking out your cabin room once again, honey. Are you all right?"

"Papa, I'm so afraid!"

"All aboard!"

The steamboat blew another splitting whistle in the evening air. It muffled the wild laughter in the gambling room and quieted the roustabouts on the deck.

"Come, walk with me to the gangplank," Jeremiah said. "Why are you afraid, Malindy?"

How could she explain that the boat would lose all its excitement when he left, leaving only her memories of her mother's death and the runaway slave?

"There's nothin' to be afraid of, Malindy. The captain's a good man. He's been on the river a long time and knows it well. He's promised to deliver you safe and sound to Eliza at the Mobile dock."

All the same, Malinda's throat ached. She changed the subject. "Is Aunt Eliza like mama?" she mumbled.

His arm tightened around her. "There's nobody like your mama, Malindy."

"Then I reckon I better go with you."

Jeremiah put his big, strong hands on her shoulders. The shock of black hair falling over his forehead did not hide the ache in his eyes.

"Malindy, gal, we've been over this again and again. Your mama wanted you to get some schoolin'." His gaze roamed her face as if to etch it in his memory. "I promised her years ago that we wouldn't let the move west keep you from gettin' it. Neither one of us forgot; we just couldn't let you go."

"You can teach me better than anybody."

"You're almost grown up, child, but you need a mama for a while yet. Anyway, this wilderness is too hard a life. I'll go on farther west, find a place, and clear some land. I'll come for you when the time is right."

"But, papa, I can help you clear the land."

"Malindy, we both made a promise to your mama."

Her misery pushed her on to say, "Then you come with me." But she knew he could never be happy in Mobile. All those townspeople would crowd him too close. He was a trapper and farmer, always pushing farther west when too many settlers moved in. Tomorrow he would begin his trek west with the few cattle and hogs left after paying for her passage.

He was right. They had been over and over the decision in the three months since mama had died. There was no turning back now.

"Papa—"

"Did you bring any of your stones from the ocean?" he interrupted.

"Yes." She had placed most of them at the foot of mama's grave.

"It pleases me you brought them."

Malinda tried hard to smile. "And you're takin' your fiddle along. You promised."

"Malindy—"

"I can see you goin' through the woods hollerin' and singin' and playin' your fiddle to drown out the blue jays."

"My fiddle is for happier days."

"Running Bull would like it."

His hand clenched around her hair. "Nobody can outholler a Choctaw Indian."

She looked up at his rich brown eyes, his high cheekbones, and his firm mouth, once so accustomed to smiling. "You sure did outstubborn Running Bull, or he would have never been your friend."

Papa's eyes crinkled in remembered pleasure. "That old mule! I'll never forget him stoppin' us on the Georgia trail. He got us safely across Creek Indian country, too."

"He wouldn't have, though, if you hadn't outbluffed him."

"How was I to know it was a game? That's one time, Malindy, your pa did the right thing without knowin' it. Did you know old Chief Pushmataha once took a lighted torch in his hand and invited a white man to join him on a keg of dynamite?"

Malinda smiled. It was her father's favorite story.

"What bluffers those Choctaws are! And now Running Bull is out west somewhere in another forest."

"If you holler and fiddle loud enough, maybe you'll find him again."

"Is that what you want?"

Malinda nodded. "You won't have mama and me travelin' with you this time." She could hardly bear to say it. "But if he hears you comin', he might even find you."

Jeremiah held her face and kissed her forehead and then each cheek. "I'll try, Malindy gal, I'll try."

"You can do it, papa."

"All aboard!"

"She's amoving," someone shouted behind them.

"The plank ain't up!"

Papa hugged her roughly. The boards beneath them shuddered.

"You're going to make it. You're going to come through on the other side," he whispered in her ear. "You're all I have, Malindy, and oh, how I'll miss you!"

He ran down to the landing just before the gangplank was raised.

"Stoke her up, boys! Stoke her up!" someone encouraged the firemen at the furnace. The paddle wheels began to turn, and the boat moved slowly into the current.

Malinda gripped the rail with both hands until they ached. She could see papa on shore in the twilight, his hands deep in his pockets. He was still standing on the landing when the steamboat passed around the bend.

Malinda gazed at the now blurry tree-lined shore and tried to remember everything her father had said... "You're going to make it." If only she could believe that, too. Once she was at Aunt Eliza's perhaps she would not have to go into the hated woods again. She clung to the thought; it eased the pain of leaving papa.

She had not always been afraid—only since that frightening night alone in the forest, the night mama died. In the three months since, she had not stayed by herself in the cabin or walked alone in the woods.

"What's got into you, Malindy?" papa would ask. "I've taught you all I know about these woods, and you can't get lost in the daytime. You know everything I've learned from the settlers and from the Choctaws. So how come the devil rides you every time you step foot out there?"

Finally one night she broke down and told him what had turned the woods into her enemy.

"God have mercy on their souls," papa had whispered. "Why didn't you tell me about the runawayer before now?"

"I couldn't."

"You rest on me and try to forget."

But she could not. And soon he began making plans for her to go to Aunt Eliza's.

It was a sleepless night. The bed was so tiny that Malinda dared not turn over for fear of falling out. Whenever the fiddlers struck up a familiar tune in the main cabin on the other side of her door, it recalled painful memories of the times her parents had danced to the same music.

The songs and shouts and boisterous laughter and sometimes the crying of a young child on the deck below also reached her. This night was nothing like ones at home where in the stillness she often heard a hoot owl or coyote or a lone wolf cry.

To escape the sound—and the memories—Malinda slipped out the other door, bringing her directly onto the upper deck to watch the passengers below. Flaring torches on rods extended out over the water. Papa had said that sometimes they were used to guide the pilot through a black night.

Restless, she returned to her cramped sleeping quarters.

She picked up an ivory-handled hair brush, the only possession of her mother's she had brought. Slowly she brushed, her head tilted sideways—the way she and her mother let their amber-brown hair fall to their waist. She had mama's hazel eyes, too, and a spattering of tiny freckles across her cheekbones. Papa had said she was going to be as pretty as mama. She hoped so.

Then she thought of her father. Tomorrow he must face the wilderness alone.

3

A NIGHTMARE OF FLAMES

BY THE SECOND NIGHT on the *Alabama Queen,* fatigue and grief had overwhelmed Malinda. She fell across the tiny bed without bothering to undress. She even felt feverish.

That did not surprise her. It must be one of her "upsetting fevers" as mama called them. They would come unexpectedly—such as the time Aunt Eliza left on the ship and when she and her parents uprooted their home in North Carolina and headed west. Or whenever father was away for several days to sell animals or pelts or to buy supplies.

The fever could vanish just as quickly. If she

gave in now to her drowsiness, perhaps tomorrow it would be gone, and several more hours of this lonely trip would have passed.

Malinda awoke choking and coughing. Smoke was suffocating her like the times she tended fires and a wind change engulfed her in heavy smoke. Frantically she snatched open the door to the deck and gasped for breath.

An explosion rocked the *Alabama Queen,* sending the rear section up in flames. The fire spread quickly to the bales of cotton stacked seven or eight tiers high. Passengers spilled out onto the decks, screaming and cursing. They jostled Malinda as they ran past.

The tortured face of the runaway slave ared out at her from the flames. His image emed as real as the frantic passengers on the boat.

The entire steamboat would soon be in flames. She did not board this vessel to be burned alive like that runawayer. She scrambled wildly over the rail of the upper deck to the top tier of a bale of cotton, which was just beginning to topple.

She jumped.

She did not think once that the river was wider and deeper than the creek behind the log cabin at home, that her skirt and petticoats would tug like undertow, or that she might be hit by burning cotton bales toppling over the sides.

She thought only of escape.

Water closed in around her. She dragged one arm over her head, pulled the other down, then drifted with the current in quick exhaustion. The water in her ears muffled the cries of others and the crackling fire. She was enveloped in another world that tugged at her.

But she would not let herself drown, either. Her legs kicked in slow motion. Slowly her chin rose above water, and she inched toward the distant shore.

An overwhelming splash deluged her, but she thrashed to the surface again. Heat burned her face. Flaming cotton bales hissed as they hit the water not three feet away.

She was dragged under by the current. *Don't fight it! Set the rhythm!* Did her brain still function or had someone shouted? But those were her father's words.

Malinda Sharp! Malinda–she stretched her limbs as she sounded each syllable. *Sharp*–she kicked her legs together, pulled with her arms. If she could remember her name, maybe its rhythm would be her salvation. *Malinda*–she stretched. *Sharp*–she kicked. *Malinda . . . Sharp!*

Her hands finally struck roots. She pulled herself up but fell exhausted half in the marsh, half in the river's edge. Water gurgled in the grass under her ear.

Shrieks slashed the darkness, and Malinda tugged at her water-soaked dress and struggled to her feet. She bogged her way through the swamp grass to the cypress tree. Then she zigzagged deeper into the woods, fleeing from what seemed to be the runaway's image rising in the flames of the steamboat. Slowly her wet skirts twined around her legs, and she fell.

Were those footsteps crashing through the forest after her? The woods were haunted with her nightmares of the past; she staggered to her feet and spurted ahead. She must find a planter's house in the bottoms. Vines whipped at her like a cat-o'-nine-tails, and she fought them off as she stumbled on.

Looking back she saw nothing but darkness and fog slithering in among the tree trunks. Muscadine vines plaited the giant foliage overhead together, sealing in the oppressive October heat. Malinda slipped on brown pine needles and wrenched sideways to catch her balance. Frogs croaked somewhere in the bogs, and a distant wolf howled in the darkness.

She turned all the way around and sobbed in terror. The river had vanished! The fog and the black night yielded nothing. No cultivated fields. No trails in the undergrowth. No cabins. Nothing.

Panting, she wiped her face with her wet skirt in an attempt to gain control of herself. Where was she? And where was the *Alabama Queen?* The dark woods were worse than the flaming ship. She ran to escape them. She tripped over vines and fell again.

Why not give up? She felt her eyelids close, locking out the night's horror.

When she awakened, she would be back home. Mama would be churning and papa trapping or fishing at a creek in the backwoods. When he came in, mama would feed them all to bursting. Then papa would make the fiddle croon a tender love song while mama sat at his feet. Later he would swing into foot-tapping music that would send Malinda reeling round the room. And then strike the minor tone of a ballad or a slave melody—a tune that pushed out at the darkness beyond the firelight in their cabin.

The scene changed abruptly. In her dream Malinda was pounding on the door, imploring someone to open it so she could join the song and the firelight. Mother was inside to teach her the steps, and father's gay tunes would turn their cheeks rosy . . . if she could only reach them. But they did not hear. She continued to pound on the door as fingers of the night reached out to grab her.

Her cry as she beat on the locked door of her dream awoke her. Scrambling to her feet she tore through the brush to escape her nightmare. Although her arms were stretched out ahead, they did not protect her. When her head crashed against a low oak limb, she folded to the ground as if into her mother's soft feather cushion.

While she slipped in and out of consciousness, she thought she heard cowbells across the meadows back home, then the soft music of lullabies, until daylight and night were the same in their passing.

PEBBLE TEA

SOMETHING INSIDE MALINDA stirred. Her eyelids fluttered. Her fingers moved, and her nose twitched. She smelled woodsmoke, and rolling over, she stared at the small fire in the center of a ring swept clean of leaves and scrubs.

Beyond the flames a face stared back at her. It was a black face, and she knew this was no dream.

"Are you a ghost?" she demanded, struggling to rise. Her weak arms and legs did not respond.

The face did not answer.

"I got to know! Are you a ghost?"

"I ain't no hant! But if you wants to get out of here alive, you better not yell again!"

"How come?"

"You find out soon enough."

"I want to know now!"

"Wait till your feeblements be gone. We is safe here."

That was strange. What was this Negro doing with her? Why didn't he take her to the big house to be cared for? She wanted out of these woods.

Malinda forced herself to stare across the fire. The face did not look black now but burnt rich brown, like the crusted sugar in the bottom of mother's cane syrup jug. The lips were still, expressionless, but the eyes commanded her attention. They were large and round as walnuts, midnight black, and they glanced at her briefly, then flicked away.

He stood. A homespun shirt and pants covered the strong body that was not much taller than she. Her heart thumped wildly as she tried again to sit up.

"I be back." He turned away from the fire and walked deeper into the woods.

Malinda could not look through the trees. The Negro might not be a ghost, but the woods were still haunted, of that she was sure. She struggled to sit up, her gaze darting around the campfire where a rack made of reeds held dried apples. Nuts and acorns filled two large gourds. Another gourd had been carved flat like a frypan, and smaller cupped dippers were near by.

Suddenly dizzy, she lay back on the bed of moss under her. How long had she been here? These supplies had not been gathered in a day. And where had the young man gone? Had he abandoned her with only a few nuts and apples? If only he would come back.

Before long he did.

"Drink this," he said.

Should she or was this some poison? But the apples and nuts, the moss bed and the fire— surely they were evidence that he had cared for her. She leaned on her elbow and took the gourd he held out. It felt cool in her hands. Inside it were water and several stones.

She glanced up at the large walnut eyes.

They avoided hers. "Pebble tea for your fever. I think it be the yellow fever!"

Oh, mama, no, no, no! She swallowed the cool liquid and stared at the smooth stones in the bottom of the cup.

The dark hands took the gourd, and once more the stranger slipped away into the forest. Malinda felt in the pocket of her dress, but her ocean stone was missing. She hid her face in her arms.

When the stranger returned, he placed the dipper of water on the fire and resumed his position across the flames.

Malinda could not stand the quietness. "What's your name?"

The face looked uncertain. His eyes darted to and fro like a hummingbird and soon focused on the dark green leaves of a jasmine vine. "Jasmine. . . . My name be Jasmine."

"A girl! Are you a girl?"

A corner of the stranger's mouth twitched. "I be a woman!"

"Oh, I'm so glad! My name's Malinda Sharp."

"I knows."

The pebbles in the gourd clattered as the water began to boil.

"How did you know my name?"

"You say it for days—Malindy . . . Sharp . . . Malindy Sharp—like you gonna forget it if you quits."

"*Days?*"

"It been ten days. You last out the fever ten days, so you gonna live."

Malinda shook with chills and sank back on the moss, too weak to do anything else. Tears stung her eyelids.

It was morning when Malinda awakened

again. The black girl was cooking over the fire. Jasmine, she said her name was, but Malinda knew better. She glanced over at the jasmine vine, remembering the sweet scent of its white flowers in spring. From the olive family, mama had once explained when she placed a bouquet in the center of the supper table.

"Jasmine?"

"Is you awake already?"

"I didn't hit my head here, did I?"

" 'Course not. Nobody hits their heads in a good hidin' place like this."

"I don't understand."

"This be a good place. Deep enough in the woods and close to a spring."

"Why didn't you take me to the big house?"

The long slender hands stirring the mush were still.

"What big house?" she finally asked.

"Don't you live around here?"

"I lives right here in this spot!"

"How long?"

Jasmine pointed to a pine. The bark had been cut away in ten short lines.

"Ten days?"

Jasmine nodded.

"But you said I had the fever ten days."

"That be how long I lives here. After we eats this mush, I'm gonna add a line for today."

"Where do you live, Jasmine?"

"Here!"

"Then where did you live?"

"My mercy me! I thought I couldn't wait till you gets over that fever. But there was blessings. I sure don't like questions."

Malinda lay back, her head swirling. What secret did Jasmine know about fevers? They had tried every potion for her mother but water—that was fatal everytime. Malinda sucked in her breath, and the other girl turned at the sound.

"Was . . . was that water you gave me?"

"No! It be pebble tea, boiled and boiled. It save you from the fever."

"Is the tea different from water?"

"Ain't you never seen tea?"

Tea. The kind that arrived on the steamboat too late for mama.

"Of course, but this pebble tea didn't change color."

"Just you never mind that. When you gets fourteen years on you like me, then you knows tea can be a heap of colors."

Jasmine was not going to answer a direct question no matter how she worded it. "Thank you for making me well," Malinda whispered.

"Oh, hush! It was the pebble tea." Jasmine handed her another gourd full, cooled at the spring. Malinda slipped her fingers into the water, removed one of the pebbles, and enclosed it in her hand, remembering her father. This one would have to take the place of her ocean pebbles.

"Are you sure I had the yellow fever?"

"Huh! That ain't all you got. Talk about hants—you got them in your head. Such goin's on I ain't never fell across before."

Remembering mama's delirious thrashings, Malinda drank the whole gourd full without removing it from her lips.

Jasmine bent over the fire. The meal was ready: bread cooked with acorn flour, catfish, and fresh apples. Malinda was ravenous, but Jasmine gave her only small portions. She pushed Malinda's questions aside while they ate.

Afterwards Jasmine folded her hands, one on top of the other in her lap, and focused her big round eyes on Malinda. "In two days you be stronger. Then we go downriver by night."

Downriver. Mobile, where father was sending her to live with Aunt Eliza, was somewhere downriver. Two words suddenly struck like cockleburs in her mind: *by night. Travel by night.* Only a fool—or somebody pretty desperate—would travel through this wilderness by night. Her eyes wandered slowly from Jasmine's leather moccasins, up her baggy pants and man's homespun shirt to the bridge of her nose and the bonnet of black curls.

Malinda was not fooled. Jasmine's words confirmed her suspicions. She was a runaway slave! She must be a runaway!

Malinda jumped up. Suddenly dizzy, she steadied herself.

"I'm goin' *up* river to my papa, and you ain't gonna stop me! He sent me away, but I'm going back! You can't keep me here!"

Jasmine did not move. "G'bye," she said.

Malinda stumbled through the carpet of fall leaves and needles, setting the jays to chattering in the trees. She gritted her teeth in misery when she was forced to stop and lean against an oak to rest. Where was the river, and which direction was north? Why couldn't she think clearly? She plunged ahead, her breath coming in rough gasps.

The trees began to turn flips in the sky like buzzards circling over a carcass. She clung to a limb.

"We wait three days instead of two." Behind her, Jasmine's voice was firm. "You can't get nowhere without me, so don't try no more."

The forest closed in on Malinda as her fingers slipped from the limb. Jasmine took her arms and sat her down against the live oak.

"I loses ten good days to save you," she said. "Now you got to stay with me."

"No! Leave me alone! You're a runawayer!

They'll cut your tongue out! They'll burn you to death—"

"Last time he just beat me with a cat-o'-nine-tails."

"They'll set a torch to you! Me, too! They'll kill me for helping you!"

"He won't catch us, I tells you! Where be your papa and mama?"

Malinda turned her head away. Her ear pressed against the washboard bark of the oak until it ached.

"My mama's dead," she finally whispered. "The yellow fever. You should have let me die, too."

5

JASMINE THE RUNAWAYER

FOR THE NEXT THREE DAYS Malinda wished she could think Jasmine without adding runawayer, as if Runawayer were her last name. What was she going to do? "You got to stay with me," Jasmine had said. And Malinda wanted to. She could no more go through the forest alone than she could fly like that hawk overhead. But once they got to the river, that was something else. She wasn't going to be caught with a runaway.

Jasmine had found a good hiding place. Nobody could find them in this undergrowth. Since they had been here more than ten days without being found, they must be the only ones for miles around.

Jasmine never stopped for a minute to rest. She would climb a tall pine to gather muscadines from the vines entwining its branches. She brought in apples she had picked somewhere and stored them in a sack that looked like one of Malinda's petticoats and boiled pebble tea until Malinda figured she was fated to drown in it.

"You make me tired just watching you," Malinda said once.

"Huh! It be the fever make you tired."

"Maybe so."

"Is you strong enough to pick berries?"

"I reckon so." It would make time pass faster.

"Come on, then."

Not far from the campfire, Jasmine showed her the berry bushes. She gathered walnuts, too, to add to their horde.

Malinda would search for berries and nuts when Jasmine was nearby. But when alone, she stayed at the campfire, hating herself for being afraid. Sometimes Jasmine would go off for hours at a time—simply disappear—while Malinda clung to her moss bed and listened to every sound in the forest. Long before the other girl's return, Malinda began to watch for her through the dark woods. Jasmine always reappeared, shining with sweat and drooping with tiredness—but still watchful.

Feeling stronger, Malinda stayed up a little longer each day. Whenever she trembled with weakness, she slipped back onto her soft moss bed. Then she would lie on her back and watch squirrels chasing and leaping at one another from limb to limb high overhead. Her mind sometimes absorbed itself with Jasmine, the Runawayer, and her heart thumped hard at the thought of leaving their safe hideout.

Thinking of Jasmine reminded her of a time before mama had taken sick when night riders had broken into their clearing chasing another runaway slave. Mother had lit a lamp, sat on Malinda's bed, and held her tightly as the lamplight spilled feebly out the open door to where father stood on the front step.

"You can't go roaring through my sheds and smokehouse," Jeremiah Sharp had said in a friendly enough voice. "But I reckon my wife and girl are the only humans I've seen today."

"We didn't say no human—just a stinkin', runnin' nigger. We gonna take a look-see anyways."

Jeremiah drew himself tall like the straight pine across the way. "You might better trust my word. It's been good for thirty-five years, and I reckon it's good now. You just step your horses right off my place and be on your way."

The men threatened and grumbled. Then a muffled voice conceded, "Awww, Sharp's okay. Leave him be."

"We need help. Git your horse, Sharp, and come with us."

"Not this time," answered Jeremiah. He had stood on the step for an hour after the riders had left.

Now Malinda gazed at their campfire. She must get away from this Jasmine as soon as she could after they reached the river. Never mind that Jasmine had cared for her and had risked getting the fever herself. Malinda had seen what happened to runaways.

When Jasmine returned, Malinda was adding the berries and nuts she had gathered to the ones already stored in the gourds.

Jasmine stirred the fire to cook the fish she had brought, and Malinda tried to grind acorns between two rocks for flour. It would bring the strength back, Jasmine had said, but it only showed Malinda how weak she was.

Jasmine viewed Malinda as she worked. "You is better. Tonight we be leavin'."

Malinda nodded. "I'm ready to get to the 'Bigbee."

"How come?" Jasmine asked suspiciously.

"Maybe we'll find somebody—"

"No! You ain't gonna turn me in!"

"But I am gettin' help."

Jasmine's chin set in a firm line. "Help?" she said scornfully. "Me and you's all the help we needs."

"That's not what my mama and papa taught me."

"If you gonna talk about help every minute, I thinks maybe I shoulda left you with the fever. Here, eat this!"

They ate the fish, a few berries, and apples in heavy silence. Afterward, Jasmine began tying vines to a stout pole she had brought to the campfire that morning. Malinda helped her tie the other ends to the filled gourds. When the moon rose, Jasmine put one end of the pole on Malinda's shoulder and the other on hers, part of their supply of gourds and the petticoat filled with apples hanging between them.

"We carry more this way," Jasmine said, "and we's goin' slow." She set a labored pace through the trees, stopping often to rest but saying nothing. Finally reaching her destination, she untied the gourds from the pole and placed the supplies carefully under a log.

RIVER OF FIRE

Malinda slumped to the ground. So what if the river were near? She was too exhausted to care.

They made three trips to the log that night—slowly, painstakingly, halting, stopping. By the last trip Jasmine was carrying most of the weight. When they returned to their smoldering fire, Malinda sank on her moss bed and slept all the next day until dark.

That evening the moist air was cool and misty, clinging to their skin as if to stifle movement. Now their fire was covered with leaves and straw as if it had never existed.

They made their way one last time to the Tombigbee River. Malinda did not once look back.

ON THE TOMBIGBEE

WHEN THEY REACHED THE LOG that covered their food supply, Jasmine whispered, "Help me turn this here log over."

Carefully they tugged and pushed until it rolled over.

"A dugout canoe!" Malinda gasped. "Like a Choctaw's!"

"It sure be a canoe all right!"

"Did you do this?"

"I sure didn't! I found it."

"Then somebody lives around here!"

"No, they don't. There was a hundred years of cobwebs coverin' this boat."

"Choctaw Indians aren't here, or they would have found us long ago."

"How do you know about Injuns?" Jasmine threw a string of gourds into the canoe, and then turned to Malinda, "Is you gonna help me load?"

"I'm gonna help."

They began packing their goods inside the canoe, being careful to balance the load.

"I learned some Indian ways from papa," Malinda explained. "Choctaws and Creeks burn out logs like this for canoes."

Jasmine shrugged.

"Were you working on the canoe when you left me for hours?"

"Yep. I cleaned it up. And it don't leak neither. I reckon it will get us downriver."

Malinda stood up straight to stretch. Reaching out for a cypress trunk nearby, she ran her hands around it in both directions. A thick layer of moss grew on one side but not on the other.

That's north, she thought, holding her hand flat on the moss. If you ever get lost, remember how the Indians tell direction, her father had told her: by a moss that grows on the north side of trees. Excitement rippled through her. Now she felt less helpless.

Placing two long poles—each with a sharp pointed end—into the canoe last, they tugged it into the marsh. When the water was deep enough, Jasmine held it while Malinda climbed inside. Then Jasmine followed.

"Don't tip it!"

"I ain't!"

"This thing's goin' to dump us in the water!" Malinda cried.

"Shhhhhh!"

They pushed the canoe clumsily with the rough poles, moving it through the high marsh grasses. Soon they edged into the Tombigbee River. The current carried them along as they fearfully stabbed the river bottom with their poles. When Malinda grew tired, she laid her pole inside the wobbly canoe and took the white pebble out of her shirt pocket. Rubbing its smooth roundness with her shaking fingers, she tied it inside a knot in the tail of her shirt in case the canoe tipped.

In a sweet gum tree behind them, a screech owl screamed.

"Screech owl say somebody gonna die." Jasmine moaned but did not break the rhythm of the pole.

Malinda tried to reassure herself. "I don't care what the screech owl says. We won't die."

The owl called again and again, and Jasmine's low moan continued until the canoe had moved well downstream.

Suddenly Malinda saw Jasmine's back

stiffen as she strained ahead to listen, the pole idle by her side.

"Steamboat be coming!"

No lights appeared through the thin mist.

"I never thought we'd find anybody on the river at night."

"You think a boat stop just 'cause it night?"

"No." The *Alabama Queen* hadn't stopped.

"Well, then."

Malinda wanted to reach out and wipe at the fog that surrounded them. "I can't see it."

"It be there!" Jasmine moved her pole, directing them nearer the tree-lined shore. They nudged the canoe under low-hanging limbs where gray, crinkly Spanish moss cascaded down among the branches to hide them from the river. The sawing of insects and the gentle lap of the water against the canoe were the only sounds at first. Finally Malinda, too, could hear the steamboat making its way upriver.

Upriver. Toward home.

Malinda counted the days since she had seen her father: two on the *Alabama Queen,* three since her ten days of fever—fifteen in all. It must be the middle of October.

"Papa's gone now," she said quietly. "He's been headed west for fourteen days."

"Then why you make like you want to go home? What be at home?"

Malinda could not answer. All she knew was that she was sick for home—the way it used to be.

The steamboat was parallel to them now, but its lights did not pick them out behind the mossy leaf curtain. The paddle wheel slapped the water, and its wake rocked the canoe. The smokestacks belched black smoke into the fog. Malinda watched it out of sight. Even if she were traveling north on that boat, she would never reach home. She had no home now. Mother was dead, and with father deeper into the wilderness, he might as well be dead.

Jasmine was looking at her. "Has you got good memories?" she suddenly asked.

"Yes." She wouldn't think about the bad ones.

"You is rich then."

Jasmine's face was a blur. Malinda brushed at her eyes.

They took their poles in hand, pushed out from their covering, and headed downstream. Later other man-made sounds rose from the shore. A bell rang and a horn blew somewhere over the bluff.

"It be a hour to dawn." Jasmine was suddenly tense. "This drift's too slow."

"What's the matter?" Malinda clutched the sides of the rocking canoe.

"That was a overseer's horn calling the field

53

hands for the day's work."

"A farm can't be anywhere in these dark woods."

"Huh! He ain't a-blowing to the chickadees!"

"You said we'd hide before daylight."

"Not here! I ain't stopping ten miles to a big house." Jasmine took up the pole again, pushing hard against the bottom. The pull of the current twisted one end of the canoe.

"Watch it, Jasmine! Be content with the drift."

Jasmine hunched over. "Come on, river. Move faster!"

Daylight slipped under the mist and lifted it from their shoulders. Still Jasmine made no move to bank and hide.

"We must stop!" Malinda couldn't keep her voice steady. She wanted help from somebody, but what would she do if they ran into someone in broad daylight?

"No! We ain't gonna stop yet!"

Stubborn runawayer.

Malinda's arms sagged with fatigue. The forest looked dark and ominous. Was someone in those woods watching them now that day was dawning? A crow cawed. Malinda wanted to fold up like a croaker sack and disappear in the bottom of the boat.

Slowly they rounded a bend in the river as

pink streaks shredded the horizon as far as they could see.

"Ye ding-busted, dag-blamed females! Git outta my trot lines!"

They were caught! Malinda jerked around. Her eyes swept the river bank. There he was. Hunkered over the edge, he clung to a taut line, his face blown into a rage. A low moan escaped Jasmine's lips.

7

A FEMALE
AND HER WENCH

MALINDA STARED AT the stranger. His eyes were sunken pools in a sharp, lean face. A homespun coat and slouch hat hung on him like on a nail behind a door. Jerking a line caught on the end of their canoe, he waved his other fist at them.

"Did ye hear me? You is playing with my trotlines! Now git! I'm gonna slap ye right up into them woods. And don't poke my traps with them poles!"

Jasmine, hanging her head, did not move. Malinda leaned over to free the line. The canoe wobbled.

"You is playing with my trotlines! Now git."

"I been outsmarted by Injuns, and I done had my goods burnt up on a steamboat. But I'll be danged if I'm gonna lose my lines to a female and her wench!"

Malinda flinched. Jasmine looked indifferent.

"Git! Git! My family's got to eat. I got nine chillun to hold in the hollow of my hand—"

Malinda jerked the line free. Under the water she saw box traps built like log cabins and a live trap in the shallows, all similar to papa's. A huge catfish, spreading its bubbles over the surface, was moving away from the live trap.

Maybe she had better capture it for the nine children. Remembering how papa had taught her, she turned her pole upside down and quick as lightning speared the fish with the sharp end.

"For your trap. It's a nice one!"

"Well, I'll be a hornswoggled goose!" The man tipped his hat to the girls. "I'm mighty obliged to you."

He pulled up the trap. Malinda stretched the pole out as far as she could reach. He added the muddy-colored catfish, half the length of his leg, to the trap.

"Do you live here? Do you have a boat? We need help—"

Jasmine grunted and pushed them away

from the shallow water near the shore.

"What you say?" the man called.

Jasmine lifted her head. "She say, 'Good luck to you!' "

Malinda looked back at the stranger. He was scratching his beard. Why had she said anything? He didn't look like the kind that could help, anyway.

After they had drifted in silence for several tense minutes, Malinda whispered, "We have to stop somewhere, Jasmine. I could have eaten that catfish raw."

"We get away from him. We crosses to the other side." Jasmine set her pole in motion.

It was useless to argue with her.

The canoe moved into deeper water and floated downriver. When Malinda let her pole straight down and it could no longer touch bottom, her stomach clutched in a knot. The opposite shore seemed miles away.

Finally Jasmine exploded. "I got somethin' to say to you! You was gonna turn me over to him. I could tell by the way you was actin'! You was gonna say, 'Here be a runawayer. Let's go get the reward.' "

Malinda bristled.

"Why didn't you, huh? Why didn't you holler for help to drag me in?"

"Get one thing straight. I'll never turn you in to anybody."

"If you goes for help, that be the same as turnin' me in. You was gonna do it the first chance you got. Why didn't you force the canoe to shore?"

Malinda could have kept Jasmine from pushing them away from the trapper, but it would have been a struggle. "I don't know, Jasmine. I guess I felt beholden."

"Beholden!" Jasmine snorted. "Ain't nobody gonna feel beholden to me."

"But you said I had to stay with you because you saved me—"

"So I say it once. That don't mean I got to say it now. You ain't gonna be beholden."

"Why?"

"Because you sit there all beholden like till you burn your insides out, and in the end you call the dogs on me anyhow."

Malinda jabbed her pole into the current.

"You gonna double-cross me, do it right now! Just get!"

"You chose a fine place for your sermon," Malinda retorted. "Right here in the middle of the river."

Jasmine wiped her face with her shirttail and lapsed into silence.

Her back to Jasmine, Malinda thought about her dark face, the long lashes that framed her large walnut-shaped eyes, the stubborn thrust of her chin. "I do thank you for takin' care of me all those days."

"It ain't no thanks if you gonna get help."

"But didn't that old man think just what you thought he would? The reason you saved me was so I could pretend to be your mistis. Don't deny it! And that's just what he thought, too. So will everybody else."

"Huh! You don't know nothin'! If that old goat wasn't all tied up in his trot lines, he be lookin' at us real hard. And he see all right that I be a runawayer. He got eyes like fire."

Malinda didn't want to say that Jasmine had acted like a runawayer, too. She kept silent.

Finally they reached midstream two miles below the trot lines. The day's sun was bright in its newness, and they were alone. Or were they? Surely a thousand eyes must be watching them from the woods.

The onrush of the water twisted the canoe into a spin.

"Watch it!"

"Oh, lawsy mercy!"

"Don't fight it!"

The canoe turned two complete circles. Then the current headed them toward the opposite bank.

Jasmine's knuckles were shiny from her iron grip on the pole. "And God say, let the dry land appear," she intoned like a preacher.

"Amen!" Malinda swallowed the knot in her throat.

They were too busy keeping the canoe upright in the swifter current to speak. A mile of shore had slipped by when they nosed the canoe into a bayou where water invaded the low land far up among the cypress trees. They maneuvered between the trunks until a slow slope framed the water's edge. Surveying the land far ahead, they saw tall sweet gums and pines among an undergrowth of swamp dogwood and red maple. Squirrels barked as they leaped like a whirlwind through the branches, and overhead in a cypress, a possum stared at them with beady eyes. A fox yelped in the distance.

When they had pulled the canoe completely out of the water, taken out all the supplies and turned the boat over on top of their rations, Malinda shook her finger at the snout-nosed possum.

"That's to keep you out of our apples!"

"You go hunt for fish since you is so hungry," Jasmine said, picking up a large gourd. "I's goin' over the hill."

"Be watchful!"

Malinda followed the riverbank with her pole until she found a shallow pool where bushes hung over the water. Soon she returned to the canoe with a large trout she had speared, but Jasmine was nowhere in sight.

How were they going to start a fire? She had never questioned how Jasmine had started the fire that had burned all those days and nights. It just was. She gathered brush and dry maple leaves and pine needles to pass the time until Jasmine returned. Ravenous, she ate an apple and snubbed her nose at the possum who was now hanging by his tail. Finally she heard the cracking of footsteps as Jasmine approached with fresh clear water.

"I come across a spring!"

"I found a trout, but I didn't find a fire." Malinda drank from the gourd.

Jasmine pulled out a small leather pouch that was tied to the inside of her pants, untied the string, and displayed a piece of flint, her knife, and a notched stick.

"I come prepared this time." She made a notch on the stick with her knife and put them back in the pouch. They cleared a place for the brush and leaves Malinda had gathered, then struck the flint between two rocks endlessly until its sparks finally lit the pine needles Malinda held.

When the fire caught up, Malinda asked, "How many times before this did you run away?"

Jasmine handed her the knife to clean the trout, then got out the gourd frypan and an apple. She ate the apple down to the core and added it, sizzling, to the flames before answering, "Once."

"How far are you from home?"

"I ain't got no home."

Neither did Malinda. She shrugged sadly. "From your master then."

Jasmine did not answer.

Malinda put the fish in the pan and placed it over the flames. "I need to know. Would they be huntin' you here? Would anybody around have descriptions of you?"

"How come you wants to know?"

"I'm wondering if night riders are out for you." She shivered at the thought.

Jasmine traced the outline of a fish in the cleared space by the fire. "I's pretty far from my big house, and I got my own plan."

"You'll still need some help."

"Huh! Help, help, help! That be the only word you knows. Last time I got helped right back to my massa, and I don't need that kind no more."

They ate the fish, another apple, and some berries.

Jasmine tossed her head. "Did you ever have a wench?"

"No!"

"Next time we runs into somebody, you better act more like a mistis."

"Who says I'm stayin' with you?"

Jasmine's black round eyes looked twice as large across the fire. "I ain't nobody's slave—if I don't get caught. Even if I has to play like you is, I ain't nobody's!"

"I ain't gonna get caught with a runawayer, either. Can't you get it through your head that they'd kill us—"

"You talks so biggety! You don't know nothin'. You ain't never felt a cat-o'-nine-tails on your back. You ain't never seen a lynching."

"I don't want to hear—"

"Keep your voice down! So you don't want to hear. You don't want nothin', does you, but your ma and pa. Well, you better figure out I's all you got right now."

Malinda tightened her fist around the pebble knotted in her shirttail until her fingers ached.

"While I'm with you, we ain't runnin' across anybody," she said. "I'll see to that."

"Who say? We has already done it once."

"We'll have to be more careful."

"But if you plays mistis properlike, who gonna know I's a runawayer?"

After a long silence Malinda said, "You'd have to teach me how to act."

"Oh, lawsy mercy! I's beginnin' to wish I had saved somebody else."

"Did you have any choice?"

"Does I have to tell everything?"

Malinda felt the tension between them drain away.

Much later Jasmine said, "I remembers how turnip greens smells cooked outdoors in a big black washpot. I sho could stand some."

"And corn bread crumbled up in the pot-licker," Malinda added, savoring the tasty liquid left in the pot after the greens were cooked.

"And buttermilk!"

Malinda lay down near the warm coals. "We're homesick."

Jasmine hooted. "Tell that to the possum!"

8

STORM CLOUDS

THE CLAMOR THAT JANGLED Malinda awake set her heart pounding like an ax hitting a tree. She controlled her first impulse to spring up and turned her head unobtrusively. Jasmine was awake, too. No one stood within her range of vision, so Malinda raised her head slowly. A wiry, dirty gray-haired possum was clattering their gourds as a dozen squirrels flitted around the canoe.

She jumped up. "Go find your own nuts!"

The squirrels scattered like chickens. The possum jumped to the nearest tree and swung by his ratlike tail from the highest limb.

"Just waiting for us to turn our backs," Malinda sputtered.

A scratch sounded from inside the canoe. She raised one end, and a red squirrel with a nut in his mouth darted out. She dropped the canoe and hunted until she found the place where the squirrel had weaseled through. Jasmine clogged the opening with the frypan.

Malinda returned to the fire, which was only a bed of coals now. "Last night plain tuckered me," she said as she lay back down.

"I got a pain from restin'. I's gonna look around."

"Oh?" Malinda hesitated, then added softly, "If you happen to meet anybody, please don't act like a runawayer. Hold your head up and look them right in the eye. If you have to give your name, say it's Jasmine even if it really isn't."

Jasmine stood as if her feet had taken root. "Now you done gone to preachin'."

"You don't want to give yourself away, do you?"

Jasmine only grunted and turned toward the slope.

It was almost dusk when Jasmine woke Malinda, her hands loaded with ripe persimmons.

"C'mon," she said. "Help me."

They hid the persimmons under the canoe. Then Jasmine led the way over the slope and turned south. Crickets and red-winged blackbirds sang, and in the crevice between the hills, daisies and goldenrod bloomed. When they reached the spring, Jasmine and Malinda drank from their cupped hands and washed their faces.

"I feel as dirty as when the sweet-potato hill caved in on me," said Malinda.

"Don't your pa know how to store taters right for the winter?"

"Sure. But once when I was little, I thought if I kept diggin' in the side of the hill, I might reach the other side of the world. It didn't work."

Jasmine chuckled. "A tater hill is a tater hill. It sho ain't the doorway to the other side of creation."

Malinda nodded.

Lying flat, her dripping face hanging over the spring, Jasmine looked at her. "My name be *Jasmine!*"

Malinda raised her head, her own face dripping wet, and stared at Jasmine a moment. She didn't know what to say. They wiped their faces on the tails of their homespun shirts.

"The persimmon tree is yonder." Jasmine pointed to a tree fifty feet away.

Malinda stripped off one of her two remaining petticoats and tied a knot in one end so they could fill it with persimmons. Later when the fruit had been placed safely under the canoe, they made another trip to the spring to fill three gourds with water.

That night they cooked up a mush with persimmon pulp. It was not tasty like corn bread and pot liquor, but it filled their stomachs. Afterwards when they put out the fire with dirt and scattered leaves over the clearing, Jasmine said, "I didn't run across nobody today, 'cept a turkey buzzard in the sky. He not flap his wings while I's looking at him, so my wish gonna come true."

They turned the canoe over and reloaded it. As they pushed off between the cypress trees in the water, Malinda wondered what Jasmine had wished for.

The moon looked like a large orange ball suspended in the sky while the twinkling stars and the fireflies in the woods seemed to be kin. Wind sent crinkled leaves scuttling across the surface of the water. Buoyed by a night's experience, Malinda and Jasmine moved with the current as if on a charted course. They took cover under branches twice when other boats passed and relaxed enough to eat fruit and nuts occasionally.

Once Malinda ventured enough confidence to ask Jasmine if she had heard anything about a steamboat explosion before she had found her in the woods.

"I reckon so. I seen it."

"You did?"

"I sho did! All that noise and fire and yellin'. I knowed the world be coming to a end, and I runned lickety-split."

"Do you know if most everybody got free?"

"Not me. I's too far back in the woods, and I's not stayin' around to see. Anyways, the night be too dark." Jasmine gave her a hard look. "Has you got friends on that boat?"

"Not really. When the boat exploded, I was too scared to think. But now I keep worryin' about the others."

Jasmine brought her pole down strong in the river. "I reckon you just gonna have to leave them up to the Lord. Ain't that what they's having to do with you?"

"I reckon so. Jasmine, how long had you been runnin' when you saw the steamboat?"

"A few days."

"Where did you come from?"

"I ain't sayin'."

"Do you even know?"

" 'Course I does. I knows a heap."

"Then tell me."

The silence grew large between them. Malinda tried another subject.

"Since you must be a long ways from home, we can get help—"

"No we ain't!"

"Maybe nobody knows about you down here."

"Maybe, you say. But we got to be for sure."

"We can't stay in this canoe forever."

"I got a plan, and we's all the help we needs."

Malinda knew better. She hadn't lived for five years in this wild country for nothing.

They banked before daybreak.

The sky clouded over in the early afternoon. Darkness seeped through the milk glass cloudiness long before it was due, forcing the girls to huddle nearer the fire.

"I wish there was a way to warm both sides at once. My backside's cold."

"Mine, too. . . . Jasmine, we been together a whole lot of days, and I don't know nothin' about you."

"Sho you does. I be a good nurse for you, and not a bad cook, either."

"I mean *before*. You wasn't born by our first camp fire."

Jasmine set her jaw in a firm line. "I be

more interested in how we gonna survive on this river."

"Me, too. And I know we won't make it by ourselves—"

"Now wait a minute!"

"But I think I have a right to know something about the slave girl who saved my life."

"I ain't a slave no more! And I got a right to tell you nothin' if I don't want to."

She surely had Jasmine's back up now. She ran her fingers through her long matted hair and wished for her mother's brush. Tying her hair in a knot to keep it out of her face, she stared at Jasmine across the flames.

"We might as well be travelin', Jasmine. I'll put out the fire."

Jasmine turned away. "I's gonna warm my backside first."

They traveled several hours that third night before they heard a roll of thunder and saw a crash of lightning streak through the gloom. The wind rose, and the rumble of thunder rebounded in the wilderness. Rain fell in torrents. Firebolts lighted up chalk cliffs far ahead in the river's bend.

Suddenly the dark water turned into a monster, swirling and rising to batter everything in its path. Malinda's hands clamped like steel on the pole, trying to control the canoe.

Jasmine moaned.

Malinda yelled, "Watch it!"

The canoe twisted and pitched.

"Hold on!"

The boat capsized.

Malinda fought the frenzied, churning water to reach the surface.

"Grab the boat!" she shouted. Lightning picked out the canoe humping a wave. She struggled to reach it, then looked around wildly for Jasmine.

"Help! Help me!" The cry came from behind her. Jasmine was thrashing the water, then she disappeared under a wave. Malinda struggled against the current to reach her, straining to find her again. Jasmine's head bobbed up suddenly, her arm smacking Malinda on the shoulder.

"Help—I can't swim—"

Thunder clapped. Jasmine grabbed her around the neck, choking her. Malinda forced herself to go down deep underwater until Jasmine let go and began thrashing again. Then she surfaced, gasping and spitting. She came up behind Jasmine, slung an arm across her chest, and headed for shore.

"Relax! Don't fight!" Malinda managed to gasp. Her legs tired under the weight as she pulled at the water with her free arm. Her head went under, and she sputtered for breath. One more stroke . . . one more . . . and another . . .

When an oak limb scratched her face, she dropped her legs but could not touch bottom. Waves beat against the bank with a force that sent them reeling in retreat, and the lashing crosscurrent threw Malinda off balance. She flung out her free arm and hit the bank. Lightning laced the sky so that she could see a sheer cliff through the trees and bushes above them.

Jasmine lay limp on her overburdened arm. Malinda reached for a limb. It broke off in her hand. She fought the slashing waves, flung out her arm for another support.

"Jasmine . . . help! Take hold!"

Jasmine stirred and stretched out, clenching the oak that grew out from the cliff parallel to the raging river. Malinda pushed with her foot against the bank to boost herself over the trunk. She hung limp. How good to feel the wet ridged bark scratching her.

"Is the land flooded?" asked Jasmine.

"No. It's overhead—a hundred feet it looks like."

"We ain't gonna make it."

Malinda pulled herself up and searched for a place to climb. Her foot secure on a root, she reached for a limb above her and called for Jasmine to follow. The river hit the banks from below, and the rain slid down from above as Malinda dug into the sticky clay to find roots to grip. When she moved a foot upward, Jasmine's hands clutched the support for her own. They stopped on another strong tree trunk growing out from the bank and rested.

Able to see only when lightning slashed the storm, they groped their way upward—slipping and sliding, clawing and digging.

"Watch that bush!" Malinda shouted against the thunderclap. "It gave a little with me."

Her warning was too late. The bush pulled loose from the wet soil, and Jasmine plunged downward.

"Catch a tree! Catch a tree!" Malinda clutched her own support in terror.

The tall pines moaned in the wind. The thunder rolled. The river roared. And Jasmine crashed down the cliff, wailing.

One sound ended. Jasmine's cry.

CONQUERING
THE TOMBIGBEE

"I'M COMIN', JASMINE! Hold on!" Malinda screamed into the void. She hunted for another place to put her foot. She turned her head sideways, straining to hear, as she inched downwards.

"Jasmine—"

"Malindy—" The sound was so weak that she did not trust her ears. "Malindy—"

Then the unsteady voice sounded once more. "Go—on to the top. I'll make it."

Relief flooded her. She wouldn't climb on. She'd wait for Jasmine.

Jasmine did not call again. Malinda dug

both feet into the clay above the root support and shouted encouragement when she could hear nothing beneath her but the roar of the river.

Finally Jasmine drew near. Malinda still could not see her, but she felt her presence, heard her every move. So she searched for another root and planted her feet there instead. Then she leaned over and grasped Jasmine's hand, placing it on the root she had just abandoned.

"Pull up—there. Now there's another one a little higher."

Jasmine eased flat against the cliff and rested. "I caught on to the oak."

"The one just above the river?"

"Uh-huh."

Malinda shuddered, and when Jasmine did not stir for some time, she said, "You lead now. I'll stay below."

Jasmine moved, reached upward to a scrub, dragged her feet higher, and dug in where a tree root corded the bank. Malinda followed.

By the time they reached the top, the rain felt matted to their eyelids. Clay and soggy leaves plastered their bodies. They crawled on their knees to the base of the nearest pine, collapsing onto the solid earth and retching for breath.

"Scree—screech owl—were right," Jasmine

gasped after a long time. "Death's a-comin'."

Malinda heaved, feeling blended into the soil and soppy pine needles. Her body shuddered with each gasp. She could not think beyond that moment.

"Death's twistin' my—breath out and—"

"Save your strength!" Malinda warned.

Lightning crackled and thunder rolled.

"Malindy! My plan done gone. I was goin' to Mobile—to stowaway on a boat."

Malinda pushed her straggling hair back from her face. Where could Jasmine go, and what would happen to her? Surely it must be hard to slip unseen onto a boat.

Jasmine lay still as death. In panic Malinda leaned over and pressed her ear against her back and was finally rewarded by hearing her breathe.

"Jasmine, we—are you hurt?"

"Scratches."

"Where do you hurt?"

"Just scratches."

Thank God she was alive. Malinda rested her head on her arms, her body oblivious to the rain pelting it.

"My rib bones aches. I thinks they's fr-freezin'."

Malinda lay an arm across Jasmine to warm her cold rain-soaked body. "You're getting your breath back."

She raised her head as lightning lit the sky. Then she stared and squinted her eyes, rubbing them with a fist in disbelief. She shook Jasmine's arm. "I saw a cabin—ahead of us."

Jasmine looked up.

"Straight ahead!" Malinda peered into the darkness until a lightning streak appeared again.

"There be more than one," Jasmine said. "I see lots."

"I can't. Come on, lightnin'."

"Let there be lights in the firmyment!" Jasmine intoned, but the flashes came less often.

"Come on! We're gettin' out of the rain."

"No! I ain't goin' to no cabins."

Malinda sneezed. "There's no light in any of the buildings. We got to see if they're deserted."

Jasmine struggled to her feet. "Oh, lawsy mercy, I don't like this." She followed well behind Malinda. "If anybody be there, I's runnin'!"

The first structure they came to was a windowless double cabin with a breezeway porch between. Malinda eased up the steps onto the breezeway, then to a door that hung crazily on its hinges.

She peered inside the cabin. A crude wood bed frame draped in cobwebs was all she could see. She motioned to Jasmine to come inside.

Malinda worked with the door until she got it latched upright while Jasmine stumbled around the room. Aided only by occasional lightning through the cracks between the logs, she found three dusty quilts heaped in a corner.

"Let's stay here, Jasmine. This settlement must be abandoned—there's no lamplight or woodsmoke. I feel no life; at least nobody is in this cabin."

"We need to shake the earth out of these." Jasmine held up the quilts.

Malinda unlatched the door, and they took the quilts to the porch and shook them until their arms ached. Jasmine winced. "My side don't feel too good," she said.

They choked on the dust. The wind and rain blew through the passageway making them lose balance and setting their teeth to chattering. Malinda sneezed and coughed again.

Jasmine stopped short, suddenly alert and tense. "Did you hear a groan?"

"It's just the wind in the trees. C'mon!"

"Mebbe. Mebbe so."

Once inside Malinda again latched the door. They rung out their clothes and hung them over the bed frame to dry. Malinda unknotted the white pebble from her shirt. Holding it in her hand, she curled up in a quilt to sleep.

Favoring her left side, Jasmine clawed at a cobweb, the lightning through the cracks highlighting her body. Then she rolled up in another quilt beside Malinda on the floor.

The storm raged overhead, but Malinda began to feel warm inside the blanket. With a roof over them and the coziness of four walls, she began to doze.

"Where was you headed?" came the muffled question from deep in Jasmine's quilt.

Malinda hesitated. Should she tell her? "I was goin' to Mobile, too."

Nothing moved inside the other bundle, but now that she was awake again, Malinda wanted to talk. She remembered the warm times at home after the lamplight had been turned out when papa and mama would share their dreams and stories of their slow trek from North Carolina to the lush lands of the West, a land flowing with milk and honey they had been told. Nobody had mentioned the yellow fever, Malinda thought bitterly, just milk and honey.

"What are you goin' to do now, Jasmine?"

There was no answer, but she spoke up again, ignoring Jasmine's silence. "What, Jasmine?"

Still no answer. She would change the subject.

"Now I know how mama and papa felt when

they had beat the forest back one more acre for planting. We conquered the Tombigbee to-night!" She felt a weary pride.

"Huh!" Jasmine suddenly grunted. "It took all our food, and tomorrow we got to build a raft."

Malinda sat straight up. "No we don't! I'm not gonna get on that river with you again. Why did you tell me you couldn't swim?"

Again Jasmine ignored her question. "G'night, Malindy."

If Malinda wasn't going on the Tombigbee again and was scared of the forest, what was she going to do? She couldn't stay here. She closed her eyes and held tightly to her pebble. She would face that question tomorrow.

HANTS!

WHEN MALINDA AWAKENED several hours later, Jasmine was sitting against the door.

"You tryin' to hold it up?" Malinda asked lazily. She bundled up tighter in her blanket.

"There be hants in this here cabin!" Jasmine's round black eyes were larger than usual. "They been groanin' and moanin', and they not like us. So we's gettin' out of here!"

"I don't believe in hants. Besides, we can't leave. It's still rainin'."

Jasmine's eyes rolled. "That don't make no difference to hants."

"It does to me. I'm sleeping another twenty

hours." Malinda moved around in her blanket, settled finally into a comfortable position, and closed her eyes. But not before she heard it—a groan as clear as if it had come from the corner of their room.

The skin on her scalp crawled. "Jasmine—" She sat up, clutching her quilt under her chin.

"Huh! Didn't I tells you?"

"I ain't afraid of hants. I don't believe in them." Her voice quavered. Her throat was dry.

"You sho don't sound like it." Jasmine pushed her back harder against the door.

Malinda flung off the quilt and grabbed her clothes, shivering as she pulled the clammy underpants and petticoat over her skinny body. She pitched Jasmine's baggy trousers to her.

"Come on out of that blanket."

The groan again.

"I'm movin' out!" Malinda jerked on the long homespun shirt Jasmine had put on her during her fever days and slipped the white good-luck stone into her shirt pocket.

"Not without me you ain't!" Jasmine jumped up and was in her clothes by the time Malinda unlatched the door and opened it a few inches. She saw nothing on the breezeway, so she eased through the opening with Jasmine right behind.

The moan sounded again, louder than ever.

"Oh, lawsy mercy!"

"Somebody's in that room." Malinda pointed to the other side of the breezeway. "Don't you think we ought to find out what's in there?"

Jasmine turned her head sideways, listening. When they heard the moan again, Jasmine said, "Is we or is we ain't a scaredy-cat?"

"We is."

Malinda stepped aside. Jasmine stuck her thumb in a knothole and pushed with the palm of her hand against the door. It moved with excruciating slowness. Malinda could hardly bear the odor seeping from the room. Jasmine held her nose with her free hand and pushed her head in cautiously, then jerked back frantically trying to get her thumb out of the knothole.

"Injun! There be a Injun in there!"

"What kind?"

"I say what kind! A Injun!"

"Let me see."

Jasmine extracted her thumb from the knothole. Malinda held her nose to block out the stench and cautiously looked inside. Heaped in a corner, as if waiting to die, was a body dressed in a printed calico shirt, buckskin leggings with beaded ornaments, and a white turban on his head.

"It's a wounded Choctaw instead of a hant," she whispered. She pushed open the door and eased over to the Indian who seemed to be unconscious. But when she put her hand on his forehead, his eyes slowly opened. His lips formed the word, "*water.*" Malinda smiled, trying to reassure him, although she wanted to retch from the smell.

"Well—" his lips barely whispered. She checked beneath his shirt and found blood-soaked rags covering his chest from just below his left collarbone to underneath his arm. She closed his shirt.

"We'll find water for you."

The eyes opened again.

"We'll be back."

The eyes closed, then opened. Was he signaling that he understood? She rejoined Jasmine. "Leave the door open to let in more fresh air."

"Where you goin'?"

"He says there's a well, so I'll have to find it. You look for something to carry water in—and dry wood for a fire. I got to find some herbs—"

"Whoa! How we knows every cabin ain't plumb full of Injuns? We's leaving and ain't coming back."

"But he's wounded and I promised. A Choctaw hates a white who lies."

"I ain't no white. And he can hate me all he

wants to. I don't trust him."

"You don't trust anybody, do you?"

"I don't have cause to trust nobody," Jasmine answered. "I's goin' and I ain't comin' back."

"Don't you trust me?"

"When all you does is talk about gettin' help and ask me more questions than tadpoles in a creek? You got to take me as me without no more questions before I trusts you."

Malinda's chin set in a firm line. "Well, I promised the Choctaw and I'm stayin'." She marched down the steps and headed north toward the well, forcing herself not to glance back at Jasmine. She would have to gamble that Jasmine would not leave without her. But she looked warily at the other buildings she passed. Grasses and weeds grew high in the pathway and around the cabin doors. There was no sign of life anywhere.

Finally she found a well located in what seemed to be the center of the abandoned settlement. A chain hung down in the well from the center pulley. She leaned over, trying to look into it, but not trusting the planks to support her. She pulled the chain up until she saw with relief that a bucket was attached to the end. She lowered it until it smacked the water below, then raised the full bucket and set it on the ground while she headed for the

"It's a wounded Choctaw instead of a hant."

woods behind the well to look for herbs.

But she stopped before she reached them. She could not go on into the forest alone. There was a chance she could find herbs for medicine in the weeds between the trees and the settlement. When she was almost ready to give up, she discovered two peach trees behind a cabin. She gathered as many leaves as she could carry in the tail of her shirt and returned to the well for the bucket of water.

It was not there. She rubbed her eyes and walked all around the well, stared at both ends of the chain that dangled from the pulley, walked around in the opposite direction, and leaned over as far as she dared to peer into its dark depths again.

Then she turned down the path toward their cabin with a sinking feeling, looking back at the well every few steps but not daring to face the question of who had taken the bucket and, more importantly, where that person might be. Were eyes staring at her through the chinks in the cabins? She shivered and hunched her shoulders. With Jasmine she had never felt so afraid.

She smelled woodsmoke! It was filtering up from the direction of their cabin. Holding fast to her shirttail full of leaves, she sprinted down the path, bounded up the cabin steps, and then stopped. Jasmine must not see how elated she was that the black girl had stayed, at least not now. Malinda walked nonchalantly across the porch and into the room where they had slept.

Jasmine was adding more wood to the fire and did not glance at Malinda. "Huh! Chickens that fly the coop always cacklin' that they be comin' back—they sho do. I bet you wouldn't a-come back if you hadn't smelled the smoke."

Malinda grinned to herself. "Is that why you built the fire?"

"That ain't for you to know."

"Look, I found peach leaves. How's our Indian?"

"He ain't my Injun!" Jasmine nodded to a cup and two crockery bowls by the fireplace. "I found them and dry wood in one of them cabins. Don't say I didn't give him some water."

"Thanks. I'm glad it was you that got the bucket at the well."

Jasmine's hand lay still on the cup for a long moment before she handed it to Malinda. "Well, don't just sit there! Get this to him."

"Okay."

Jasmine added, "I come across a crow's nest in the tip-top of a pine out yonder. So I climb up."

"Whatever for?"

"Eggs. I's looking for crow's eggs."

"Crow's eggs in *October?*"

"Well, I didn't find none, but then I remembers about birch bark, so I cuts some of that and is gonna boil it into a thick soup."

"Why didn't you catch the crow instead?" Malinda was enjoying the talk. It felt good after the scare she'd just had.

"Always wantin' something you ain't got. Now get! But first—" Jasmine turned suddenly solemn. "How does you know he be a Choctaw?"

"His turban for one thing and his long hair."

"You sure?"

Malinda held the cup steady. "I'm sure." She headed once again for the room across the porch.

11

NISH'KINHALUPA

BY PUTTING HER ARM under the Choctaw's head and holding the cup to his lips, Malinda finally got him to swallow a little water. His eyelids blinked.

"I found water, and we're making a peach leaf poultice," she said.

He swallowed again, and she set the cup down, opened his shirt, and removed the rags to get a closer look at the wound. Gangrene—that putrid odor was gangrene. She had seen enough animals with gangrene to know the poultice was too late to help him.

His eyes were staring at her, and she pretended to be busy with the wound to avoid them. He murmured slowly in his own language, his lips barely moving, but then whispered, "Too late. You come too late." He didn't sound sad.

She shook her head and said the only Choctaw words she could remember from the few papa had taught her. "Hello. I am your friend."

The man trembled and poured out a stream of low guttural Choctaw phrases. She strained to hear; he seemed to be asking her a question. She shook her head again and told him she could not understand as she gave him another sip of water. His eyes closed and again he whispered, "Too late."

Malinda jumped in surprise when she heard Jasmine behind her. She was holding out a couple of hot wet rags, torn from one of the blankets.

"Thanks, let's try—"

"*You* can try.".

Malinda turned back to the man. His glance had shifted to Jasmine.

"If you help it will be easier to clean the wound," Malinda said, but she wondered why she was undertaking the hopeless task.

Jasmine did not move. "You sure you ain't a Injun?" she asked suspiciously.

"I'm sure."

"I ain't never seen a white who could talk Injun talk."

"I have. Papa taught me just a little—"

"If your papa Injun, then you be Injun."

"Papa had friends among the Choctaws, especially Running Bull."

"How come you know Injun talk and don't know nothin' about being a mistis?"

Malinda set the cup down deliberately, aware of the man's eyes on first her and then Jasmine. "Will you please understand that my papa was a herdsman?" she asked irritably. "He lived by raisin' cattle, growin' food for us, and huntin' in the forest where a few Choctaws still live. They were his friends."

"Huh!"

Malinda's lips drew together in a tight line. "I don't know anything about bein' a mistress because we didn't have slaves, and I don't know anything about runaways either."

"You sho don't!" Jasmine snorted.

"Are you goin' to help me or not?"

Jasmine wiped her damp hands on her trousers. "I reckon so—this once."

They set to work to clean the wound, the Indian not wincing a single time but his eyes never leaving their faces.

Jasmine broke the silence. "He voodooin' us."

Malinda felt his weak pulse.

"I wish we had all them apples and berries and persimmons and the canoe we lost in the river," Jasmine whispered as if uncomfortable with the silence.

"Where's the birch bark?"

"They's boilin'. How long we got to stay here?"

"I figure this is a good rest place from last night's fight with the 'Bigbee."

"Two words you always spitting out—*rest* and *help*. I's gettin' tired to the bone of hearin' them."

Malinda grinned, her impatience gone. "*Rest* your tiredness then."

"Oh, lawsy mercy!" Jasmine stood up. "I gonna feed him and see if I can break his voodoo spell."

"Those leaves ought to soak for hours but bring them in anyway. We can't wait that long."

When Jasmine left, the man moved his hand along his right side, muttering incoherently with his gaze still tense on Malinda. Painstakingly he grasped something and moved so that she could see it. She drew back from the hatchet in his hand.

"You . . . take. You need," he managed to whisper.

She cautiously reached out and took the hatchet from his grasp, laying it on the floor behind her. "Thanks . . . thank you." After losing everything in the canoe, an Indian hatchet was welcome.

He had spoken in English again, and she wondered how much he could understand. She asked gently, "Where are we?" His eyes closed for the first time since she had begun working on his wound. She tried again, "Do you know this place?"

Mockingbirds sang in the pines.

"Ho-hobuckintoopa."

She did not know the name. "I do not understand." She waited to see if he would speak again.

"Saint Stephens."

The first capital of the state? She remembered papa saying once that it was fast becoming a ghost town, just as the circuit-riding preacher Lorenzo Dow had predicted. She had pictured Saint Stephens as being larger than this.

"Are you sure?"

"Saint Stephens," he repeated. "I . . . die . . . in Hobuckintoopa."

Malinda felt his pulse again, put the cup to his lips, and waited impatiently for Jasmine.

By the time Jasmine returned, the man was beginning to feel feverish. "These hot leaves ain't gonna do no good," she said matter-of-factly. "I's got thick soup now."

"I think his fever's risin'."

"You give him this soup so's I can hunt pebbles for tea." Jasmine looked relieved to have another excuse for leaving.

"Here." Malinda took her white stone out of her shirt pocket and gave it to Jasmine.

"One ain't enough. I hunts for more." Jasmine slipped the stone into her own pocket and patted it. "I not lose it," she said as she left.

Jasmine had been scavenging again, for cattail roots seasoned the warm soup that had been thickened with the inside layer of birch bark. Malinda fed him sip by sip. Her own stomach lurched; she could not remember when she had last eaten. Yet the stench of the wound took her appetite away.

"You look better," she observed as he finished the soup. "What's your name?"

"Nish'kinhalupa, the one with the Eagle Eye."

"Why did you give me the hatchet?"

The staring eyes focused on her. "You need it. You will go on long journey—perhaps."

"Why do you say perhaps?"

"Nish'kinhalupa sees two ways stretching out arms to you. One trail from Hobuckin-toopa follows the river to the big waters. One trail follows the sun to a plantation."

"How far is the plantation?"

"Two, perhaps three hours."

"The big waters—is that toward Mobile?"

Eagle Eye nodded, struggling to raise himself.

"You must rest. The talk is taking away your breath."

"No, I die here. The ashes of my people are here." He raised himself until he was supporting his weight on his elbow. Malinda understood how he had acquired the name Eagle Eye; she squirmed under his gaze.

"You won't need hatchet if you go west to the plantation. My people go west. Now we are broken."

She moved the hatchet from behind her to his side. Looking into his eyes, she wished she had paid more attention to the stories papa had told her about the Choctaws and Creeks who lived in Alabama. Saint Stephens had been a large trading center long before the white man moved into the wilderness. Indian trails from every direction crossed there. She also knew that most of the tribes had been moving west for several years. Her parents were guarded in what they said in front of her about the removal of Indians from their lands. But papa's face always looked bitter and grim after a visit with his friend Running Bull.

"Some of your people live a-half day's travel from my papa's cabin," she said.

"I come back to get all my people." Nish'kinhalupa lay back exhausted, beads of sweat standing out on his forehead.

"How were you wounded?"

He ignored the question.

"Six winters I am away from this land of my people." His hand clasped tightly around the hatchet. "I hear their voices. I see their tears."

Malinda wiped his face with one of the clean wet rags, then added more hot leaves to his wound.

"The plantation. Is it just two hours from here?"

His eyes seemed to stare right through her. "You take the trail west. Do you go without the slave?"

She had no answer.

"You go west, and perhaps you, too, see tears."

She nodded, goose bumps popping out on her arms when he turned the hatchet in his hand and laid it on the floor pointing south. "You know Choctaw trail signs?"

"My papa taught me."

His words tumbled out as if he expected each one to be his last. There was a good trail to Mobile, he said, but if she knew the signs she could take a short cut and pick it up farther south, thus saving a day's travel. Follow the river one day, cross a swamp, and pick up the signs southwest at the Choctaw cabin, one hour's travel past the swamp. Exhausted he fell back.

"Take gift," he added.

Malinda wiped his face again. Did she dare give him sips of water instead of pebble tea now that his fever had risen? And where was Jasmine?

The eagle eyes rolled back; his eyelids closed. "Go now," he whispered.

WHICH WAY?

MALINDA SAT IN FRONT of the fire in the cabin where she and Jasmine had slept the night before, shivering as she fingered the hatchet and waited for Jasmine to return with pebbles for tea. She turned it so that the head faced away from the river—west, toward the plantation Eagle Eye had mentioned. She wanted to strike out in that direction. Turning it clockwise, she changed the hatchet head to point south—toward the wooded trails, the swamp, the days of travel with a runawayer to Mobile.

Why should she go on downriver when help

lay two hours away? She could tell Jasmine the trail Eagle Eye had described, and even give her the hatchet so she could go on alone. Eagle Eye had said Malinda would not need it if she traveled to the big house. What else had he said?

"You go west, and perhaps you, too, see tears."

What if she did? She had seen plenty in her lifetime. She was sick of her constant fear, of cringing in the woods whenever she was alone. Besides, she was weak from hunger, and food and shelter lay only a short distance away.

Eagle Eye had never pointed the hatchet west, only south. Malinda picked it up and deliberately set it down pointing west. Then she tasted the thick soup Jasmine had left warming in a tin cup on the coals, relaxing now that she had made her decision. She handled the hot cup with the tail of her shirt and sipped the soup slowly. Holding it in her mouth until it penetrated every spot and her teeth ached from its heat, she savored each drop until it cooled. Only then did she swallow it, concentrating on the soup and avoiding a glance at the hatchet.

"What about the Injun?"

Malinda jerked guiltily, hugging the warm tin cup with her palms.

Jasmine stepped closer to the fire. "I can't find white pebbles for tea."

"We don't need them now."

"What does you mean?"

"He told us to go."

"Is we just gonna leave him to die?"

Malinda sipped slowly from the cup. "That's the way he wants it."

Jasmine slipped by Malinda and crossed the porch. She tried to peek through the knothole before she opened the door, moving cautiously toward the Indian's outstretched body.

"Malindy!"

Malinda set the cup down and joined her.

"He dead, ain't he?"

Malinda placed her hand on his forehead, his fever replaced by an icy clamminess. "He's dead."

"Now what we gonna do? With just that hatchet, we be diggin' a grave till old Joshua make the sun stand still."

"We'll leave him here."

"Right here on the cold floor? You's tetched in the head."

"That's the way he wanted it."

"How you know?"

"I just know."

"Huh!" Jasmine turned on her heels and left. In a minute she returned with one of the blankets and carefully placed it over Eagle

Eye. "You and that Injun sho don't know much about dying."

"Somebody'll come along one day and burn this place down. Then his ashes will join those of his people. It's what he wants, I tell you."

"It still ain't human. Now let's git! I ain't mouthin' off no more in this room." Jasmine bolted out the door.

Malinda looked at Eagle Eye's calm features, then stepped outside. Sticking her thumb in the knothole, she closed the door carefully. She glanced at the hatchet in the other room and on beyond it to the bed where the dress her mama had stitched by hand hung.

"Jasmine, if you knew a plantation were close by, would you go there for help?" Her voice shook as she struggled to keep calm.

Jasmine looked at her with suspicion. "Me go to a big house? How come you ask?"

"I just wondered."

"You know I ain't joinin' Daniel in the lions' den. I ain't goin' to no big house neither."

But if she went ahead and found out they were friendly, she could return with help, Malinda convinced herself. She could pose as Jasmine's mistress, and no one would be suspicious. If the folks at the big house weren't kind, she and Jasmine could follow Eagle Eye's trail. It sounded sensible, but Jasmine would never agree to it. For once she must follow her own feelings.

"I'm going to draw some water," she said quickly and walked into the room for the bucket.

"I ain't stayin' here with no dead Injun."

"Go on ahead then. I'll catch up. Eagle Eye told me how to save a day's travel." Malinda shifted the bucket to her left hand. She did not look at Jasmine as she continued.

"Listen carefully now. You need to know the directions, too. We follow the river one day to a swamp, then one hour past the swamp we'll find an Indian cabin and signs to the Mobile trail. Why don't you check along the river for a trail?"

"Why you talkin' lickety-split? Don't you remembers? The river is the trail."

"It may be too thick with underbrush."

"I give a look-see. Don't get plumb lost on the way to the well."

Once outside Malinda jumped the last three steps to the ground, splattering water and mud from a puddle over her one remaining petticoat. She would not look back as she hurried down the path between the deserted cabins. Did Jasmine suspect? "Don't get plumb lost!" she had said, and she shouldn't expect Malinda to get lost going to the well.

Malinda drew the water slowly so the bucket would not hit the sides. She was shaking as if with cold.

"Quit the quaverment," she said as she set the bucket on a plank shelf at the top. The circuit-riding preacher used to say water was the staff of life. Or was it bread?

She was not really leaving Jasmine, she reassured herself, just going to get help.

She turned and, without glancing to either side, crossed the road, skirted between two cabins, and set her direction straight into the woods. It was the first time she had been in the forest alone since the night mama had died. No, it was the second; the first time came after her escape from the *Alabama Queen*. She must not panic as she had then.

She walked under the dark pines and oaks, her heart pounding like a war drum. Little of the day's gray cloudiness seeped through the heavy foliage, but she must have several hours of daylight before it got dark. She must! Her hands, clammy with sweat, clenched into fists.

The storm had fizzled out like a slow fire, but the wind was rising again. She stopped dead still and hid behind an oak as a creak, like a sagging door, sent chills through her. Then she tried to isolate the sound. Finally she gazed upward where the trunks of two dead giant oaks rubbed together, creaking eerily when they crisscrossed in the wind.

She pressed her forehead against the washboard ridges of the oak in relief. She had come perhaps a hundred feet. Could she survive two hours more in the woods just to reach the plantation? Still, fields cleared for planting might not be far away. A dense forest did not last forever; one could stumble into a clearing without even seeing it—she had that night last summer.

She shuddered, then stepped out from the oak. For the first time, she noticed streaked scratches on the oak's surface, as if it had been clawed by a wildcat. She moved on, stumbling over a log as she searched for a clearing ahead. She would *not* jump like a jack rabbit at every sound.

Her fear tasted like bitterweed. It followed her every footstep until she could stand it no longer. She turned and fled back the way she had come.

Tears blurred her vision. The forest seemed denser. She was defeated. She would never reach the plantation and never learn to control her fear either, for she was running back to Saint Stephens and Jasmine. Storm-drenched leaves and mud weighed down her feet.

The gray cloudiness seeped in among the trees ahead. Still she ran as if she were being chased until she was out of the woods and near the row of huts by the well. There she stopped long enough to snatch the bucket and fling out the water; then she dashed wild-eyed down the road to the last cabin.

The girl on the breezeway shouted, "What got into you?"

Malinda took the steps two at a time in a dash for the fireplace, where she grabbed Eagle Eye's hatchet. Sobbing, shaking, and sweating, she raked pieces of burning logs and coals from the fire into the bucket.

"What you doin'?" Jasmine kicked a log that had rolled out on the floor back into the fire, watching her with alarm.

Malinda could not bring herself to burn down this cabin, not with Eagle Eye's body in the other side. But her only hope was to whip up a fire large enough to draw the plantation folks here to their rescue. She could not travel another step through this wild country.

"What you doin'?" Jasmine demanded.

In a frenzy Malinda headed for the door with the coals. "If you have to know, I'm goin' to another cabin—" Her voice was shrill.

Jasmine latched onto her shirttail. "How come?" She, too, was near panic.

"I have reasons!" Malinda twisted away.

"You gonna burn it?" Jasmine's voice rose to a wail.

When Malinda didn't answer, Jasmine snatched at the bucket.

"You ain't gonna burn it! I not let you!"

Malinda tried to run, sobbing. But Jasmine jerked her arm. A smoldering wood knot flipped out of the bucket onto a quilt; then the quilt puffed into flames.

They stomped it, but the fire quickly spread to another quilt lying in a heap on the floor. In panic Malinda dropped the bucket, spilling red coals out in the room. She grabbed up the hatchet and her dress hanging over the bedstead as smoke filled the room.

"You crazy!" Jasmine yelled.

"I didn't mean to—"

Suddenly the whole room seemed to burst into flames. They dashed out to the rain-soaked ground.

"The devil got you! That fire bring out the whole countryside."

"Yes yes yes! We'll get help now. It's our only chance!" she shrieked.

"It ain't mine! I's runnin' before the whole woods crawls with slavers."

Malinda clutched the hatchet. "I'm stayin' here till help comes."

"You ain't closin' me in no trap with your help." Jasmine's eyes were wild. "I's leavin' for good, you hanted witch!"

Tears spilled out over Malinda's cheeks.

Jasmine was fleeing through the pines.

"Don't leave, Jasmine," Malinda sobbed hardly above a whisper. "I didn't mean to do it."

THE VIGIL

MALINDA WATCHED JASMINE disappear out of sight, heading south toward the river edge. I didn't leave Jasmine. She left me, Malinda thought, sucking in deep gulps of air between her sobs but feeling no relief. She only felt abandoned. The white stone she instinctively reached for was gone. She had given it to Jasmine for Eagle Eye's pebble tea. She had nothing left to cling to.

She circled the cabin endlessly. There was something beautiful, yet sad, in knowing that Eagle Eye's ashes would mingle among the cabin's remains and eventually return to the

earth that had belonged to his people. Setting
the cabin on fire had been an accident—would
Jasmine ever believe that?—but it had
seemed right for Eagle Eye. He had wanted to
die in this place; otherwise, he would have
gone somewhere for help rather than burrow-
ing himself up in the corner of a cabin. Her
sobbing ceased, and a calmness and peace surrounded her. This fire was so different from
the violence she had associated with fires.

Although she was exhausted, she kept a
vigil in all directions, anticipating
someone—anyone—to be summoned by the
fire. When that someone came, she would
sleep in a warm room for days, eat until she
ached, and be given safe travel to Mobile. She
could turn her back on the wilderness forever.

At the thought of eating, the ache in her
stomach returned. Somewhere nearby she
had seen some checkerberries, so she headed
toward the well. She moved along the edge of
the pines to look for them as she had when
hunting herbs for Eagle Eye. When she found
them, she ate like a wild pig stripping the
berries, then hoarded the rest in the dress she
still carried. She gathered the bright leaves to
nibble on later.

Jasmine was probably hungry, too. She
might be running so hard she wouldn't find
anything to eat, or she might cross trails with

someone attracted by the cabin fire. Suddenly the checkerberries tasted like potash. How could she eat when she would never know what happened to Jasmine?

She stuffed a handful of berries back in her dress. The burning logs sizzled and hissed as the last of the flaming cabin sank to the ground. The milky sky darkened; soon night would settle in.

Night. A creeping fear shivered along her spine. What if no one came?

She had not considered that possibility. Stay here alone? She gazed in the direction of the river, which she could not see below the bluff. Would any river travelers pass by and find her? Surely they could see the fire.

The cry of a hawk filled her with dread.

Timbers fell and resettled as they burned, while Malinda stared shivering into the fire. The same helpless loneliness that she had felt as she watched father kneel beside mother's bed last summer washed over her.

Malinda buried her face in her hands. She sobbed for all her named and unnamed terrors, for mama and all the losses she had known, for the long months of separation from papa that now stretched out into eternity, and for Jasmine.

She blinked at the embers shimmering before her eyes.

The hatchet felt heavy in her hand. Eagle Eye had been right all along. The only trail she could rightfully follow and still live with herself was through the hated woodlands straight south—with Jasmine.

There seemed to be enough woods to test her a hundred times over. Papa had said she could not run from the wilderness and survive, and mama had said it was in the wilderness that one found God. All she could say right now was that she and Jasmine needed each other.

She shivered, chills like a creepy crawling vine moving through her again. The hissing flames seemed to be the only noise in all the woods. The birds had stopped singing; no winds rustled through the trees; no squirrels skittered from limb to limb.

She juggled the hatchet in her hand. "Thank you, Eagle Eye, for the hatchet," she said aloud to the flames. "And g'bye—as Jasmine would say."

The fire no longer evoked images of a runaway's torture and that was a good omen as she moved away from the heat.

The forest seemed as deserted as ever. She darted through the pines toward the river. It was not a question of could she find Jasmine. She must find her.

The pines grew right up to the riverbank. She glanced quickly over the bluff and wondered how she and Jasmine had ever climbed to the level ground in that vicious storm.

She kept her gaze out toward the river as she ran on the soggy pine needles, trying not to think about the woods around her. The bluff continued as far downriver as she could see, past the white cliffs she and Jasmine had viewed from the canoe.

The bend in the river seemed endless. Pains pinging her ribs slowed her pace, but soon she was streaking through the trees again, realizing that the twilight was disappearing. She found no trace of Jasmine. She wanted to call her name into the darkness, but she did not dare.

She tangled in cobwebs and stumbled on roots. A hoot owl called from the dark recesses of the forest beside her. A fox yelped. Tonight there would be no moonlight. How long before total darkness? Malinda moved blindly ahead, her chest aching, her throat closing tight.

Suddenly she heard a bell ringing. People were shouting. Lights were visible far below on the river. A large boat was pulling away from shore. Ahead a moving line of slaves carried supplies away from the river as their masters waved and shouted back to the boat. How long had they been hauling supplies, and where were they going? Had they stumbled on to Jasmine? *Oh, God, where is Jasmine? If you have anything to do about it, God, don't let her get caught!*

Malinda ducked behind a tree. As she slid down to the ground near a bush, she toppled over a body hunched up in a knot.

TOGETHER AGAIN

MALINDA HUGGED the soft brown body. "It's me—Malindy," she whispered in her ear. "Don't be afraid."

Jasmine pulled away. "I ain't scared!" she whispered in contempt. "There they is, the help you always cryin' for. Now git!"

"Hush! You want them to hear us?"

Jasmine fell silent. Malinda waited. Several minutes later she whispered, "Maybe they've gone. I'll take a look."

"Hush! I hears voices."

They strained to hear.

". . . girl lost. What'd cap'n say the name was?"

"Sharp, was it? Yeah, Sharp. Only passenger unaccounted for, eh? Probably drowned."

"Cap'n's passing the word along up and down the river. As a favor to her old man, he says."

The voices dwindled away into the forest.

Malinda's blood pounded. "Did you hear that?" she whispered.

"Sho I did. What you gonna do?"

"We're gettin' out of here lickety-split. They know I was travelin' alone on that boat."

Their glances met and held.

Jasmine finally said, "I wonders if they knows it all down the river."

"There goes our help, Jasmine. We don't have any hope for it now."

"But, Malindy, all you got to do is follow them voices. Tell them who you are, and they get you on a boat right down the 'Bigbee to Mobile."

It sounded tempting.

"And what would happen to you?"

Jasmine hung her head. "I made out all them days before I find you. I reckon I can get to where I be goin' without you."

Malinda had never heard such loneliness in Jasmine's voice. "I reckon I better stay with you. Now, come on! Follow me."

Jasmine stopped her. "You ain't acting like

no hanted witch now, Malindy."

"No, I'm just myself."

"You sho you ain't doing this just 'cause you feels beholden?"

"How could I feel beholden? You'd have been drowned long ago if I hadn't pulled you outta the river. I figure we're even."

Jasmine grinned. "I remembers. Okay, then I follows you."

Malinda raised slowly so she could see over the bush, hidden by the darkness that had enveloped everyone. She remembered the Choctaw movements papa had once taught her—the games she had played with him, disappearing instantly and turning up minutes later somewhere else without his detecting her.

She inched along on all fours for several feet and then stood straight as an arrow behind a pine, waiting several seconds before looking out around the trunk. She motioned for Jasmine to follow, then stooped and crawled off to the left and flattened herself beside a log. If he were watching her now, Running Bull would have roared his approval.

Jasmine joined her, copying her same movements. "I can't stay here," Malinda whispered. "Let's stoop low, keep our direction by the river, and go as far as we can."

"What if they's dogs around?"

"Did you hear any before I found you?"

"Nope."

"Let's go then." Malinda moved out from the log. They ran stooped over until their backs and legs ached, then flattened themselves on the ground and rested. They heard only the quietness of the forest.

Sometime later they straightened up behind a live oak tree, its huge craggy limbs covering them like an umbrella. "Let's sleep here," Malinda said on impulse. "We can travel faster at dawn."

"We ain't too far from back there."

"Don't you think we're safe for now?"

"I reckon."

"Let's fox any snoopin' dogs." Malinda led the way far down the trail and then doubled back to the giant live oak.

"Don't touch the tree trunk, and our scent will end way down there on the trail."

She swung up on a low broad limb with Jasmine following her. They walked the limb and climbed to another higher one and yet another until they each found huge comfortable forks to support them for the night's rest.

Malinda passed the berries to Jasmine. "For you."

Jasmine ate in silence; Malinda liked the sound.

Finally Jasmine said, "G'night, Malindy."

It sounded as if she was glad they were back together. Malinda smiled up at the black sky.

"G'night, Jasmine."

Malinda was awakened by Jasmine pulling at the tail of her slip. "I's got a feeling dawn's a-comin'."

Malinda yawned. "We hardly got a mite of sleep."

"We better eat these berries so's you can put this dress on."

"First meal we've had together since before the river storm," Malinda said sleepily. "The Lord's been good to us."

"Uh-huh." Jasmine paused, then added in a tense voice, "I asks you, does you reckon the Lord intended for some peoples to be slaves and other peoples free?"

"I reckon not, Jasmine. Why?"

"Well, the preacher what comes to my massa's, he always tellin' us the Good Book say God made us slaves, and we gotta stay slaves. We preordered, or something like that."

Malinda held her breath. Jasmine was telling her something about her past life.

"If it be so, then we's goin' against the Good Book's preachments."

"My papa read us from the Bible every night," said Malinda. "But he never read anything like that. Maybe your preacher—"

"He ain't *my* preacher!"

"Mine neither. I can't believe God preordered mama to die from the yellow fever, so I reckon I can't believe he preordered you to be a slave either."

"You better hush that kind of talk."

"You started it."

"Good! Then I's stoppin' it."

Malinda stretched stiffly, slipped off the shirt she had worn over her slip, and pulled her dress over her head. It hung looser than when she had last worn it. Now it was all grubby and berry-stained. She touched the folds of the skirt and the lace on the bodice, remembering how pleased she had been when mama first tried it on her. She tied the shirt around her waist.

Jasmine was digging into her pants pocket. "Here. I reckon you wants this back." She dropped a white stone into Malinda's hand. "I's sorry not to find pebbles for tea for that Injun. Reckon it coulda done him good?"

Tears blurred Malinda's eyes. "No, Jasmine."

"But I not look too hard for them pebbles."

"That's not the reason he died."

Jasmine was gazing at the smooth white stone. "I hope not," she said. "I sho hope not."

Malinda tied the stone up in a shirt sleeve

that dangled from her waist. Reluctantly she said, "Dawn will catch us soon. Let's go."

As they descended along the oak limbs, they heard a bell far in the distance.

"Time to get to the fields," she whispered. "Let's run fit to kill."

They traveled quickly to put as much distance as possible between them and the boat dock they had passed the night before. Intent on their watchfulness, they seldom talked. Malinda's guilt over leaving Jasmine yesterday was replaced by a relief that she could not explain or understand.

The day turned into thick, muggy heat, an aftermath of the storm. By late morning the moisture in the air felt like a physical force the girls must penetrate.

"It isn't natural," Malinda said, wiping her face with the shirt tied around her waist.

"That sun be pullin' up the storm and flingin' it at us all over again."

The bluff wasn't so high now, and before them it sloped easily to the river. They raced ahead, left their clothes on an overhanging bush, and slid silently into the cool water.

"Just don't whoopity 'round!" Jasmine said, ducking under the water.

By midafternoon the heat was oppressive;

no breeze gave relief. Just when Malinda thought she could not walk another step, she saw the swamp Eagle Eye had mentioned, swimming before her vision like a mirage. The river ahead curved like a snake.

"We can cross the swamp like Eagle Eye said and cut off several big bends in the river," she said.

"We goes straight across like the crow flies—if the canebrake ain't too thick."

"Let's try," Malinda said. If she was going to conquer the forest, she might as well keep at it until she dropped.

The canebrake, a swampy land covered with bamboolike cane, was thick enough to give them firm footing as they started across. But Malinda did not like the boggy unknown under her feet.

"Are you afraid we'll see water moccasins?"

"I just see cane grass below and that devil sun above," said Jasmine.

By the time they reached midway, Malinda decided it would have been faster to follow the riverbank. She had never known such stifling heat even in midsummer. Suddenly a droning noise pricked their ears, and a cloud passed under the sun. They stared in horror as the cloud moved swiftly across the swamp.

"Skeeters! Skeeters!" Malinda sobbed. "Run for your life!"

SKEETERS

By THE TIME they reached the riverbank on the other side—fighting and scratching and flailing at the mosquitoes through the tough canebrake, vaguely aware of the danger of broken cane stobs that could go right through a foot—the cloud of mosquitoes had devoured them. The whine pierced their brains as if they could never rid themselves of it. The mosquitoes' lifeblood was theirs—coming off on their hands as they wiped at their arms and beat the air in front of their faces. They scrambled up the sloping bank into the forest, and the swarming insects veered off out over the river.

Then by instinct Malinda and Jasmine turned back to the river and fell into the water, dunking their heads and swishing their hair about to get the mosquitoes out and wiping away the blood and insects from their bodies. Out on the bank they whimpered like pups and packed mud on their skin to take away the sting. They helped each other wring out their wet clothes and sobbed in their weakness.

"Under your eyes," Malinda gasped and patted mud high on Jasmine's cheeks.

Jasmine picked at mosquitoes still lodged in Malinda's drenched hair. Their eyes met.

Exhaustion squeezed Malinda's chest; her legs trembled. She shivered in her wet clothes but was devoid of feeling—suspended and numb. When was it ever going to end? The fear that had stalked them—the pain and agony and guilt in all their running? Her gaze clung to Jasmine's for support.

A wave of depression enveloped Malinda. She looked down at the mud in her hand.

"Jasmine! Your foot's bleedin'."

Jasmine had long since lost her moccasins. Malinda dropped to the red clay ground.

"Skeeters didn't do that." She turned Jasmine's foot and found the gaping wound on the underside.

Jasmine's eyes widened. "Cane stob, I reckon. But it not be hurtin' bad till now."

Malinda tore out the back of the shirt Jasmine had given her and cleaned and wrapped Jasmine's foot. She must not think about the torn wound or what lay ahead, or she would give in to nausea.

"I still hear the skeeters in my head," she whispered as saliva ran fast in her mouth.

Suddenly Jasmine whimpered, and Malinda glanced behind her. The cloud of mosquitoes had turned on the river and was heading back in their direction. She grabbed Jasmine's hand and Eagle Eye's hatchet, and they scrambled—haltingly this time—back up the slope and into the woods.

She felt beyond nausea and tears now—beyond despondency and fear. She knew only that she must not stop, that she must place one foot in front of the other, that she must hold on to Jasmine. When Jasmine faltered, Malinda held her arm so that Jasmine could hobble on one foot, then supported her as she hopped. Later, looking behind to be sure the mosquitoes were not on their trail, they stopped and rested—too weak to say anything. The only thought that held Malinda together was the hut: Eagle Eye had said a Choctaw hut lay an hour beyond the swamp. Never mind that the swamp now seemed six hours behind them. The hut must be there, and it must still be unoccupied.

Finally Jasmine rose, and they continued, the heat oppressive under the foliage but still hardly penetrating their consciences. The hut drew them on. It seemed their only hope on a trail that held out no hope, no assurance at all.

When they finally reached the hut, they could do no more than stoop and enter the low doorway as if it were as familiar to them as home. They fell exhausted across beds covered with cane shucks and slept in a stupor.

When she awoke, Malinda's gaze canvased their refuge, seeking out the light through the doorway and the holes at the top of each gable. As her eyes adjusted to the darkness, she discovered Jasmine across from her on another cane bed.

"Jasmine!" she whispered urgently, alarmed that she was outsleeping her for the first time. There was no answer.

The cane shucks rattled as Malinda dragged herself up and placed her feet on the dirt floor three feet below the bed. She swallowed, her throat feeling tight and raw. By the time she reached Jasmine, she was exhausted, but she placed her hand on Jasmine's forehead. It was hot and dry. She pulled her gaze away from the serene face; she must find water—and a poultice for her foot—and food. But first of all she needed containers, and the strength to carry them.

She found utensils in a corner of the hut: a pottery bowl and a pot, a gourd dipper, a wooden spoon, which looked recently used. Neither were the ashes in the round circle of stones old. Was it Eagle Eye or someone else who had built the last fire?

She must keep moving for Jasmine's sake. Jasmine had saved her life once. It seemed so long ago. . . . Now Jasmine needed medicine and food, and she must not fail her again. She stooped as she moved through the low doorway to the bright sunlight, she herself feeling alternately flushed and chilled.

It took three torturous trips to bring the clear spring water, the apples, checkerberries, ground ivy, and cattails to the Choctaw hut. While Jasmine still slept, she finished gathering dry limbs and leaves for a fire. Suddenly dizzy, she leaned against the mud wall, too weak to make another move.

The fire, Malindy. You must start the fire, she was telling her dulled senses as she shuffled over to Jasmine and retrieved the flint from the pouch tied at her waist. It seemed to take forever to get any sparks.

Put the water on, Malinda implored herself grimly. She bruised the ground ivy leaves as the water boiled in the pot, and soon she had a poultice for Jasmine's wound. In another container she made tea with the checkerberry leaves.

Jasmine moaned and awoke as Malinda was wrapping her foot with the hot poultice. Neither spoke until Malinda was finished.

"Now some tea," she said gently, bringing the dipper to her.

"Pebble tea?"

Malinda could not lie. "No. But mama used this kind for aches and pains."

Jasmine turned away.

"Please, Jasmine. You need it for strength." She supported her, raising her enough so that she could sip from the dipper. Malinda's arm trembled with her weight.

Jasmine's eyes above the dipper studied her carefully, and when she lay back down, she said, "You is sick, too."

"It's the skeeters," Malinda said.

"Is we safe here?"

"Eagle Eye thought we'd be."

Jasmine's eyes closed. Before Malinda had finished an apple, Jasmine was asleep again. Malinda ate another apple and some berries and drank some tea. She woke Jasmine and held the dipper for her once more.

"Thanks," Jasmine mumbled.

As she crawled wearily back on her cane

bed, Malinda was silently joyous. Her sick fear of the woods, worse than the sickness, had clawed and beat at her outside the hut. But she had thought of Jasmine's face on the cane shucks, pretended Jasmine was walking beside her, and talked aloud to her for courage. Best of all Malinda had forced out the strength to move, to hunt, to carry, to nurse; and if she must, she could do it again tomorrow.

TICKLING TROUT

THE NEXT TIME Malinda awoke it was dark, and Jasmine was boiling cattails over the fire.

"What you doin' up?"

"Don't you talk biggity to me just 'cause I had the feeblements." Jasmine stirred the cattails and then hobbled over to her with the gourd dipper. "Drink!" she commanded.

The gourd rattled suspiciously. "Where'd you find the white pebbles? I couldn't."

"When you really needs pebble tea, you finds the pebbles."

Jasmine put the dipper to Malinda's lips. Beads of perspiration clung to Jasmine's forehead, and her hands shook.

"It's your turn. Drink it all," Malinda likewise commanded.

Jasmine hesitated only an instant before she raised the dipper to her own lips. Returning to the fire, she sat cross-legged and slumped for some time before checking the cattails for tenderness and removing them from the fire.

Malinda joined her, also sitting cross-legged. "You need to lie down and stay off that foot."

Jasmine ignored her, lifting cattails out of the boiling water with two sticks stripped of bark, which they used for stirring. When the cattails had cooled in the bowl, she popped one in her mouth and handed one to Malinda.

"Sho would taste good in chicken stew," she said.

"I could fix a trap like papa's for a rabbit or squirrel."

"No, you is too poorly."

Malinda stuck her chin out defiantly. "I am not!"

"Don't blaze up like a kindling fire," Jasmine admonished. "We not need meat bad enough to tucker you plumb flat." She shook with chills although she tried to control them.

"I'll lie down again if you will," Malinda said, trying to crack Jasmine's stubbornness.

"You's the one that needs it."

They finished off the rest of the cattails, reveling in them despite the flat flavor. Then they ate fruit and drank tea from the dipper.

"If you not rest unless I does, I reckon I will," Jasmine finally admitted and hopped to her cot.

Malinda smiled wearily to herself and fell asleep as soon as she lay down, her hunger halfway satisfied for the first time in days.

The next day a coolness tinged the air, sweet relief from the storm's oppressive heat. Each girl had risen in the night to tend the fire and give the other sips of pebble tea. Malinda put another hot poultice on Jasmine's wound. Now that it was daylight, she was determined to make a trap and snare meat for a special feast.

She had not been wielding the hatchet long, however, when she was forced to abandon the project, tears of frustration and fatigue blinding her as she checked to see if Jasmine still slept. The least she could do was catch a fish. She could imagine Jasmine's joy in waking to the smell of smoking cat or trout; it might make her forget chicken stew.

As she considered how she would make the catch on her way to the river, Malinda's memory flashed back to a time when papa had first taken her to the creek.

"You master this old Indian skill, and you'll be the best fisherman around before you're knee-high to a grasshopper." Papa's face had crinkled in pleasure.

"As good as you, papa?"

"Heap better than me," he had said. "But you got to be still like a sleeping alligator for this one."

He had taken her to two logs that extended out over the creek—"I placed them here just to try this trick." When they were stretched out flat on them, papa had said, "Now dangle your hand down beside the log, and when a trout comes along, tickle his belly. He'll lie so still you can grab him right out of the water."

Malinda had laughed. "How will we get the trout to come by?"

"We wait. Most of fishin' is waitin'."

They had lain on the logs two hours, past mama's dinner bell. When she had finally found them, she laughed, too, and tumbled papa right off the log into the water. Before their water fight was over—in which they both were soundly dunked—Malinda had decided they had scared the trout off anyway; so she had joined in the frolic.

Stretched now on a pine freshly fallen into the Tombigbee River, Malinda smiled to herself. Papa's patience had finally won out. Later, when he brought in trout he had tickled into submission, mama had admitted he was not just joshing her with a tall tale. But she had always teased him about it.

Now Malinda dozed in the sunshine, and when a turtle nibbled her fingers, she caught it and walked as fast as she could back to the Choctaw hut. Turtle soup would be the first, and only, course for their feast.

"I thinks I has you figured out. You could have left me for good back yonder, but you didn't," Jasmine said later as they drank the soup. "So I reckon you ain't leavin' me no more."

It was not a question, but Malinda nodded anyway.

"But you ain't stickin' to me just for *me,*" Jasmine added firmly. "You got another reason."

The soup suddenly tasted like mud.

"And you want me around to pretend to be your mistress if we're caught," retorted Malinda.

"So we's two of a kind? Huh!" Jasmine's voice regained some of its old fire. "With them boatmen's tootin' your name up and down the Tombigbee, you ain't nothin' but a millstone around my neck."

"Are you sure?"

"I reckon." Jasmine's fevered face faltered.

"Well, just as long as you just 'reckon' and aren't dead sure, I guess we'll get to Mobile together."

"You *guess?*"

"I know."

Jasmine carefully examined her as if desperate to read her mind.

"Does you think your papa is turned around from the West and huntin' you?"

"I don't know. I can't get my hopes up, so I won't let myself think about what those men said. But I've been thinkin' about my mama and papa. Do you want to hear how to be the best fisherman around?"

Jasmine only grunted, but Malinda told her everything she had been remembering all morning about tickling trout.

Jasmine's laugh began deep in her throat, musical and rich like honey in a honeycomb. "I's glad that turtle come along."

"You just wait. I'll get you a trout yet."

"Ramble on, child. Ramble on."

17

SOME ANSWERS

THE NEXT DAY both girls felt stronger, although each had pushed beyond their limits to nurse the other. Their fevers were waning, and they ate better. Thanks to the hot poultices and Malinda's care, Jasmine's wound was beginning to heal, but she could not yet put her weight on the foot. They were still weak enough, however, that neither girl had suggested that they leave the security of the hut for the southern trail.

They kept a fire going night and day for warmth and to keep animals away. The bowl and pot were turned upside down over nuts, fruit, and berries when they slept. The squirrels, coons, and possums were evidently satisfied harvesting from the same trees and bushes for they seldom bothered them. Occasionally they heard a fox yelp or a cat scream in the distance, but the ancient hut with its mud walls covered outside with cypress bark protected them.

One day Malinda lay again on a pine, which had fallen out over the river. She was determined to catch a trout by tickling its belly. She dangled her hand into the shallow water and rested. Ever since the mosquito attack, every bit of energy used meant twice as much rest was needed.

Waiting for a fish would give her time to figure out how she was going to ask Jasmine some questions.

She lay there, half sleeping in the morning sun as minnows nibbled at her fingers. She almost missed seeing the first trout, and the involuntary jerk that brought her mind back into focus scared it away. The next time, she vowed, she would be more alert.

Malinda concentrated on the murky water below her, straining her senses as she kept awake by going over again the little she knew about Jasmine.

She was determined to catch a trout by tickling its belly.

Then the ripples in the water below her increased. Slowly, gracefully the large light-streaked body moved toward her.

She held her hand and body still. Even her breath came infrequently and only in a steady rhythm. Now she could see the tail and belly close by her hand. Carefully she stroked the soft under portion with one finger. The trout lay still, suspended in the water and time.

Quickly Malinda turned her hand over and grabbed the trout, locking him in from above with her other hand.

The trout thrashed up and down, but Malinda held on, raising it out of the water and carrying it quickly back to the cabin.

She greeted Jasmine, who was by now awake, not with an abrupt I-told-you-so but with the joy of someone who has a treasure to share, one that would ease the vague ache of hunger that still permeated each day.

Once the trout was cleaned and cooking on a rack over the fire, Malinda began changing the bandage on Jasmine's foot with a clean piece of shirt.

Finally she asked, "Jasmine, where are your mama and papa?" Her heart pounded for fear she would not answer.

Jasmine stopped cracking the nuts they had found yesterday under the walnut tree behind the hut. "Your face be still swoll up with them skeeter bites. You looks like a squirrel with two handfuls of nuts in her jaws. . . . I ain't got no ma and pa."

Malinda bent lower over her task. "Are they dead?"

Jasmine resumed her nut cracking. "You done gone to meddlin'."

"I told you about my folks."

"You sho did! You was so feverish back in them woods you not know who you was talkin' to."

"I also told you about them when I wasn't feverish."

"Will you finish wrapping that foot so's I can move this rack off the fire properlike?"

"No!" She could be as stubborn as Jasmine.

"That trout you tickled to death gonna burn to bits. . . . No they ain't dead, I reckon."

Malinda waited.

"My massa sold them away when I was a young'un, no more than two."

"Why?"

"Oh, lawsy mercy, I hates meddlers." Jasmine rolled her black eyes toward the mud roof.

"Are you huntin' your mama and papa?" Malinda persisted.

"Huh! It be easier to find a pinch of salt in a flour barrel than find them."

Malinda had finished with the bandage, but

she still held Jasmine's foot.

"Well, don't look so sickly," Jasmine snapped. "And so I has no remembers, good or bad, of my folks. Ever since I was knee-high to a gnat, I been sewin' on lace and ruffles for my mistis and her gals. And so now maybe I got a man, and this fish am burnin'.'" She pulled her foot away, turned and poked at the fish smoking over the hot coals.

Jasmine had shared more than Malinda had dared hope for. Her mind was reeling with the information. Was Jasmine married, and where was her man? And what was she doing on the run like a wild rabbit?

Feeling that she would burst out with dozens of meddling questions that might keep Jasmine from sharing again, Malinda picked up a pottery bowl and disappeared out the door.

"I'm going to the apple tree," she said.

Malinda awoke long before Jasmine the next morning, with a prickly wariness like a cat's fur rubbed the wrong way. For the first time, she did not feel safe in the hut. Had the skeeter fever and the Choctaw shelter taken away her watchfulness? Or was it because she had discovered well-trodden trails, crisscrossing in all directions, not a mile away?

She had ventured farther away than usual yesterday, looking for the Choctaw trail signs and testing herself against the strange, hovering forest. Alone and out of sight of the hut, she pushed herself beyond her dread until she happened upon the well-used trails too near their hut for comfort. The discovery sent her scurrying back to Jasmine. Now she fussed inwardly everytime she rustled the cane shucks beneath her. They scratched at the silence.

She bolted out of bed. There was no silence now. The birds had seen to that.

"Jasmine! Wake up! Somebody's comin'."

Jasmine did not move, but she was breathing heavier. "Don't hear nothin' but jays squallin'."

"That's what I mean. They're warnin' us."

"Since when the jays start talkin' to you?"

"Never mind. I just *know*. C'mon, we can't stay here." She kicked dirt over the hot coals before they stooped cautiously through the low entrance, looking first in all directions.

"Listen!"

"Somebody's south of us—away from the river."

"Maybe it be a bobcat?"

"Papa said you can trust a jay, and they're sayin' it's a human comin'."

She headed up the river, back in the direction they had come a few days before, with Jasmine hobbling along close behind. The sound of pounding hooves sent them scurrying behind a clump of holly bushes. When voices sounded in the distance, Jasmine whispered, "We got to figure how to get out of this here pickle."

Ah! Jasmine had said "we."

"We can sit still as a Choctaw for hours if we have to." Malinda tried to sound reassuring.

Suddenly a call broke into their whispering.

"Howdee! Howdy there!" The horses were trotting closer again. The voices were clearer.

"Let's poke around a mite. 'Twasn't no hant built that fire."

"You fan out that away, Jess. I'll go up river. If all's clear, we'll just help ourselves to some vittles."

"Oh, lawsy mercy!" Jasmine made no sound, but Malinda read her silent lips. They crouched lower to the ground, the squirrels barking in the treetops adding their warnings to those of the jays. Then a horse sounded nearby. It snorted as it passed them, moving on north.

"Anybody could hear that racket," Malinda whispered later as she wiped clammy hands on her sleeves. "He's headin' away from the river now. Maybe he won't come back this way."

Again they heard voices.

"Howdee! Anybody home?"

The girls shuddered. Malinda resisted the urge to run farther upriver.

"They's back at the hut."

Malinda nodded and slumped. "Now we wait."

It seemed hours but must not have been much more than one when the riders returned to their horses and took off west from the river. The girls raised only high enough to gaze through the holly leaves.

"Now we go."

"Not yet. They might be tryin' to flush us out by pretending to leave."

The squirrels quieted, the jays disappeared, and the girls relaxed. Malinda pulled off a dozen holly berries and stared at them as she rolled them in her hand.

"Jasmine, how old are you?"

"I told you long time ago. I's fourteen."

"I forgot. I'm twelve."

"Maybe so."

"I was born in 1824."

"Mistis say my ma and pa was sold in 1824."

Perhaps she would answer another question. "Are you married?"

The silence made Malinda shiver.

"I got a man."

"But—"

"Well, I jump over the broom with a man, but my massa took him away."

"You what?"

"Let's go back to the hut now."

"No, we have to wait longer." Malinda gazed at Jasmine's brooding face. "Jasmine—"

"It say in the Good Book that the Lord don't like pushers."

"You sure don't like them." Malinda vowed once more not to question her again, knowing full well she would the next chance she got. She turned away and threw the berries one by one toward a hollow log several feet away.

Suddenly Jasmine chuckled. "Look at you! Face swoll up like a chipmunk, hair tangled like a thicket, shirt half tore up for my bandage. And that dress now—you's just about fit for a boggle-eyed coyote!"

Malinda ran her fingers through her hair. "You could stand a little fixin' up yourself."

"You got a nice laugh, Malindy. I ain't heard it in a long time."

"So what are you butterin' me up for?"

"It ain't no butter; it's the truth. But I got another truth—we better not stay in that hut too long. We was just plain lucky this time."

18

BACK ON THE TRAIL

AN HOUR LATER, carrying the pottery bowl, pot and dipper, and all the foodstuffs they could handle, Malinda and Jasmine left the Choctaw hut, following close to the river.

If only we weren't so weak yet, Malinda thought. *If only Jasmine's foot were completely healed.* They moved slower than before, but Jasmine did not complain as she hobbled along. In the lead Malinda stopped often for them to rest.

"If the moon shine tonight, let's keep goin'," Jasmine said the next time they stopped, crouching under a tree.

"What does your foot say about it?"

"It say, lead me to Mobile." Jasmine chased an ant with a twig. "You want to hear about my man, Malindy?"

She would hear anything freely offered. "If you want to tell me," she answered.

"I reckon I's huntin' him, and I gonna find him, too."

"I hope so."

"I made myself a promise, Malindy. I's dead sure I gonna find him, then him and me's gonna be married properlike."

"You aren't married?"

Jasmine's eyes flashed like lightning. "Sho we's married, but we just jump over the broom. That ain't like massa done for all the others."

"The others had the preacher?"

"Sho they did. Whenever the preacher ridin' by, massa snatch him by the coattails and drag him in. And he do up the whole thing with the Good Book, nice and solemnlike—pretty, too—and then everybody have eatin' and dancin'." Jasmine stood up. "I's rested now. Let's git."

They walked side by side.

"Oh, massa give us partying all right. He laugh his fool head off and say we can jump the broom. Jeb say in my ear after we done it that when preacher come, we get him to do it up proper. Then we dance and sing and eat most all the night."

Jasmine stopped suddenly and scowled. "I hears a boat."

"I hear a bell ringin', but it's far away." Malinda's gaze scanned the river. "I see a big steamboat. It's on the other side."

"Ain't it fine that river be so wide?"

"I didn't think so when we were crossing it in the canoe. But yes, it's fine."

"Malindy, a whole big bunch belonging to massa jump over the broom," Jasmine said as if their conversation had not been interrupted. "But later the preacher always take care of them."

"Maybe your master was going to do that for you and Jeb, too."

"Huh! You's just fooled! When all the party be over, Jeb just disappear."

Malinda stared at Jasmine.

"Come on! Don't stumble on the root, or I has to carry *you*," Jasmine warned; then she continued, "He just disappear like a hant."

They sat on a log to rest and watched the steamboat, Jasmine talking so low and fast that Malinda leaned nearer to hear. "Massa lock him up and trade him off like a hoss—"

"Why, Jasmine, why?"

Jasmine hung her head. "Massa say I too pretty for my Jeb."

"Do you know where he is?"

"Sho I knows. After he be sold he runned away, and he get word to me that he go north."

"Where?"

"Well, I can get there by boat. I runned, too, after that, but I be scared of my shadow—"

Malinda could understand that. "And you tried to get help and got sent back home—"

"Uh-huh."

That night they built a fire back in a bayou and rested till dawn, Malinda dressing Jasmine's foot and feeding the fire, their only protection from the cold. At best it kept them only half warm.

Malinda could not sleep. She suspected that Jasmine did not know for sure where Jeb was. She was probably running away from her master as much as she was hunting Jeb and freedom.

"Jasmine, you asleep?"

"I reckon so!"

"Do you still have a plan to find Jeb?"

"I find him, and nobody gonna stop me."

Malinda gazed up through the pines at the harvest moon and realized she was just as afraid of the forest now as when she first vowed to conquer it. Despair gnawed at her stomach and filled her with dread.

An owl screeched in the woods. Jasmine groaned, flames from the fire flickering on her face. "That screech owl howlin' death?"

"They have to screech sometime. I guess he doesn't know we're here."

"I believes you, maybe. G'night, Malindy."

"G'night, Jasmine."

KNEE-DEEP INTO
NOVEMBER

BY LATE THE NEXT AFTERNOON Malinda
realized that the fever from the mosquito attack had taken its toll; their pace was too slow.
Jasmine could not make it to Mobile on foot
until her wound healed better. But the
weather was turning against them; she had
felt winter coming in the chill of the last few
nights. If they stopped for a few days and the
nights turned bitter, how could they survive
with no shelter or warm clothes?

Jasmine was gathering cattails by the
river. "Looky at all the logs washed up on the
bank. That's a good sign, ain't it, Malindy?"

"It looks like our storm at Saint Stephens hit here, too. The waves churned up a lot of loose stuff, I guess."

"I like that. We be usin' it."

"It's too wet to make a fire."

"I knows that," Jasmine added gently. "I got other plans."

"Maybe I can catch a fish to eat with these cattails. But let's keep goin' till near dark, Jasmine—that is, if you feel like it."

"I feels like it."

Soon the ground rose away from the Tombigbee. A drizzling rain began, but they pressed on and soon reached a bend in the river. Malinda's throat tightened as she stared across the water.

"We'll have to walk two miles around this bend just to get over there," she said grimly.

"I reckon we can make it there before we stop."

As they followed the curve of the river, Jasmine's face brightened. "Looky! All that brush on shore." She pointed to the opposite bank.

"So what?"

"Malindy, let's hunt for a good stoppin' place in this here bayou. Tomorrow we's headin' for that brush."

Malinda plodded on ahead, too tired to figure out why the logs and debris washed up on the shore excited Jasmine. Wishing the bank sloped gently from the water instead of rising so sharply, she leaned over the edge and looked down at the water ten feet below. She noticed a path through bushes growing out from the cliff and on impulse scrambled down, holding on to branches for support. Halfway down to the water, she found a cave and called softly for Jasmine to join her.

"It's not really a cave," she said, "but it's big enough for you and me and a fire."

"I's ready to move out of this rainy drip. I'll get the fire stuff, and you get the fish."

After Jasmine's foot had been redressed and they had eaten fish and boiled cattails, Malinda gazed at the drizzly black nothingness outside their shallow cave and measured her words carefully.

"I've lost count of the days, but it must be close to November. How much longer will the warm weather hold?"

"I ain't lost count." Jasmine pulled a stick from her pants pocket. "This here's nicked mighty near to pieces. We's knee-deep into November, not chin-deep, mind you, just knee-deep."

Malinda studied the stick Jasmine handed her, counting the nicks aloud.

"That be every day since we leave on the canoe. I can count, too," she said proudly. "Can you read?"

Malinda nodded. "Not a lot, but papa taught me all he knew. That's one reason he put me on the boat for Mobile—so I could go to a real school."

"What be the other reasons?"

Malinda averted her eyes and tried to smooth out the wrinkles in the once beautiful dress her mama had sewed for her. She had never had many clothes, but mama saw to it they had something clean to wear every day. Malinda and papa had kept up the washing the same way after mama died.

"My mama ordered this piece up by boat from Mobile," she said. "She sewed it last summer just before. . . Well, it was the last thing she did, and now look at it."

"You still got it, ain't you?"

"Yes, I still got it."

"Now, don't change the subject on me this time. I wants to know how come you never talks anything bad about your ma and pa. Was they angels from heaven?"

Malinda stirred the fire with a stick, flicking ashes away so the coals could flaunt their bright colors. "No, Jasmine, but now you've gone to meddlin'."

"Ain't meddlin'. I's tryin' to help."

"Why do you think I was askin' you questions? I was tryin' to help, too."

Jasmine poked the other side of the fire. "I reckon so."

"Anyhow, I can't remember anything but happy times, before last summer." Her voice, hoarse with emotion, lowered to a whisper. "And last summer I want to forget—if I can."

"I believes you not want to talk about it yet."

Tears rimmed her eyes at Jasmine's words. Would the day ever come when it would not be too painful to talk about mama's death and papa sending her away and her terrible fear? She could not imagine it.

"We got room enough to lay down." Jasmine surveyed the space on her side of the fire and promptly curled up as if to go to sleep.

"G'night, Jasmine."

"Oh, I ain't goin' to sleep. I's just gettin' my body satisfied so's I can tell you we got to make a raft tomorrow."

"You wouldn't dare get back on the river!"

"I sho is."

"Deliver me from a raft when you can't swim."

Jasmine snorted. "Deliver my feets from walkin' trails."

"A slow trail's better than drownin'."

"Malindy, you knows we ain't gonna make

it on foot. I feels winter creepin' in, and pretty soon me and you's gonna be cold, like lard chunked in spring water."

"I won't get on the Tombigbee again."

"We can build a raft tomorrow and get on our way after dark. It be savin' days, Malindy."

Malinda didn't answer, wanting to reject everything Jasmine had said and her own doubts about Jasmine's stamina.

"Me and you ain't dressed for out-and-out winter, Malindy."

"We ain't prepared for the 'Bigbee, either."

"We gets prepared."

Malinda curled up on her side of the fire, trying to avoid further discussion of a raft. "Jasmine, if Jeb really loved you, why didn't he come back and help you escape with him?"

Silence.

"Jasmine?"

"I's runnin' my mind on it, but I can't catch no answer. He musta tried." Jasmine rolled over, her back to the fire and Malinda.

"Is you askin' how come your pa left you if he loves you?"

Silence.

"Malindy?"

"I didn't think I was, but sometimes I wonder."

"I reckon me and you's in the same boat."

Malinda was silent for a long time.

"Is you asleep?" Jasmine asked.

"No. I'm tryin' to remember something mama told me once. She was talkin' about how someday I'd grow up and be independent from her and papa."

"I reckon that's right and proper."

"And I said no—never! But didn't she miss grandma and grandpa? And, Jasmine, she said—now let me remember just right." Malinda stared long into the fire, then repeated her mother's words. " 'Love doesn't depend on time or place, honey. They love us in North Carolina, and we feel it away out here on the Tombigbee.' "

The coals sizzled and popped. The rain outside the shallow cave crackled the fallen oak leaves, and a light wind rustled the trees.

"I reckon that be our answer, Malindy, if we needs a answer. Jeb, he love me right where he is."

"And papa, too."

Jasmine thumped her chest. "I got a feelin' right here about Jeb and your pa."

"What's that?"

"I feels they's tellin' us to use our common sense to build that raft and get back on the river!"

PREPARING FOR THE
'BIGBEE

THE NEXT DAY'S SUN was bright and warm.
Malinda and Jasmine had risen at dawn and
now were busy sorting out limbs from the debris by the riverbank and hunting vines to tie
them together for a raft.

Jasmine wiped her face and looked at the
sun. "Today be pretty nigh perfect."

"It's a good thing, because you're goin' in the
water!"

"Who say?"

"You did! You said last night we'd get prepared for the 'Bigbee, and that means you
have to learn how to swim."

"Oh, lawsy mercy!"

Malinda chopped at a limb with Eagle Eye's hatchet. "As soon as we get this raft put together, in you go."

Jasmine walked down to the edge of the river and peered in as if to challenge its depths. Suddenly she put a hand up to her face, feeling along her cheekbones and down her hairline to her jaw and chin.

"Malindy, I is pretty!"

"You're smart, too."

"Reckon I can go to school?"

That was a new idea to Malinda, but she nodded anyway. "And I can teach you a little about letters and words."

"Smart and pretty. With that I don't need no swimmin' lessons."

They hacked notches down the sides of two limbs. Several hours passed as they hunted for the right size of limbs for the crossbars and vines to strap them into the notches. By midafternoon, however, they floated their small raft with pride and exhaustion.

When they banked the raft, Malinda reached down and picked up a handful of smooth rocks in the edge of the river. She swished the sand off in the water and spread them out in the palm of her hand.

"Aren't they beautiful?"

"Every color of the rainbow and then some," Jasmine responded.

"Do you think they'll ever get to the ocean? Or maybe that they're kin to the pebbles that wash up on the ocean beach?"

"You is mighty serious, Malindy, but I sho don't understand you."

"I don't either, Jasmine. There are so many things I don't understand. I never heard of pebble tea, but those stones got me over the fever."

Jasmine hesitated as she started to get off the raft. "I suspects it be more than just old pebbles that make you well."

"Did you ever wonder if the stone you held in your hand was once a star?"

"Not before now. . . . Is you gonna save these stones, too?"

"I don't know."

"I keeps them for you." Jasmine tipped Malinda's hand and poured the rocks out into her own, pushed each one with her index finger, and then stuffed them into her pants pocket. As she did so, she began singing softly:

My head is wet with the midnight dew,
    Come along home, come home.
The mornin' star was a witness, too,
    Come along home, come home.

By nightfall Malinda had taught Jasmine

how to stay afloat in the water by paddling like a dog. First she had her hold on to the edge of the raft while she kicked with her feet and legs, then came the paddling with her hands and arms until at last Jasmine decided the water could help hold her up rather than drown her.

"It ain't easy!" she said with a note of triumph in her voice.

With the swimming lesson completed, they washed their clothes at the edge of the river, scrubbing the dirt and stains with sand. Malinda had always sprinkled sand over the floor at home before sweeping it. If it could get floors clean, it would help their clothes.

"Do you think the sand will clean us, too?" Malinda began rubbing some on her arms.

"We sho could stand something."

When they had rubbed themselves all over with the wet sand, they jumped back into the water. Malinda dived under and when she surfaced, Jasmine splashed her in the face. That was all it took to get a water fight underway—a cautious water fight. They did not shout or laugh, only chuckled.

What fun to play! They had almost forgotten how.

Finally they lay exhausted in the shallow water, their heads cradled by their crossed arms on the sand.

What fun to play! They had almost forgotten how.

"Won't it be fun someday, Jasmine, to shout so loud all creation can hear us?"

"I never knowed what fun it be when I do it anytime I want."

"Mama and papa and I used to have water fights in our creek. I bet you could have heard us for miles."

Jasmine chuckled. "We chilluns used to get cooled off in the waterin' troughs in the pasture. The cows and massa not like it a bit, but it sho was fun."

"And someday we can sing loud enough to fill up the whole forest."

"Sho enough?"

"Yes." Malinda brooded. "You know, I don't like the woods."

"That be strange. You live in them all the time."

"I liked them when Running Bull made his turkey gobble ring through all the trees."

"You talk about that Running Bull before. Who's him?"

As they lay at·the river's edge at twilight, Malinda told Jasmine about Running Bull, the Choctaw who became papa's friend.

"Where he find him?"

"On the Georgia trail. Papa had packed all our belongings in a wagon in North Carolina, and we moved west, papa fiddlin' the whole way."

"He not too smart to fiddle through Injun country."

"He said he couldn't sneak by the Injuns, anyway, so he might as well warn them that Jeremiah Sharp was comin' through. He was goin' to the 'land of milk and honey' and wanted to sing about it. And everything was all right, too," she added, "until one day when a turkey gobble filled up the fog ahead of us."

"What be that?"

"It's an old defiant Choctaw call. Then a howl sounded through the forest. Papa howled back. 'I can't stand not to answer,' he said with a grin. An Indian with a fiddle under one arm appeared from nowhere and blocked our trail."

"What happened then?" asked Jasmine.

"Papa carried on a starin' game with the white-turbaned Indian. Finally the Indian said, 'My land don't need another fiddle in it. You go back to the land of your fathers.'

"Papa didn't blink an eye or say a word. Neither did the Indian. . . . Finally papa shouted, 'Every land can stand another fiddle.'

" 'Foolish man do not know Running Bull's fiddle,' the Indian replied.

"But papa didn't answer, only stared.

" 'Running Bull melt your bones down for fat.'

" 'Jeremiah Sharp cut your flesh up for blubber.'

" 'Running Bull make you swallow a thousand-pound gourd so you rattle when you walk.'

" 'Jeremiah Sharp make you swallow a thousand-pound bull to go with your name.'

"After that exchange the starin' seemed to last forever. Then Running Bull began to chuckle. When his rumblin' laugh filled up the distance between them, papa began to laugh, too."

"Lawsy mercy, he be lucky."

"Two stubborn men!" Malinda laughed. "Running Bull joined us on the wagon, and he and papa tried to out-fiddle each other all the way across Georgia and Alabama to the Tombigbee River."

"What happened then?"

"Running Bull wouldn't let papa settle on the east side of the 'Bigbee. He said that was Creek land, so we must join him on the west side—Choctaw country. And he stayed not too many miles from papa's clearin' until last year. If he could learn a thing or two about fiddlin' from papa, he said, papa could learn a lot about farmin' from him."

Finally Jasmine said, "I hopes your pa find him out West. Even a man need a friend in the wilderness."

"Because of Running Bull, I had to help Eagle Eye. Do you understand?"

"I does. I hopes we help our Injun. We sure not make him well."

Malinda smiled. Jasmine had said "our Injun."

They carried the pebbles in their hands and their wet clothes on their arms when they walked back to their hideout on the other side of the bayou. Now they could barely see as twilight gave way to night. Malinda realized she had hardly noticed their surroundings all day except as they yielded materials for the raft. The pines seemed larger than they had this morning, and a live oak's black limbs under its green coat seemed to stretch with knotty pauses into eternity.

"We worked quietly today, didn't we?"

"Uh-huh. Why?"

"We were so far back in the bayou I forgot to watch out for people. Could anybody have seen us?"

"No. We just naturally watches out without even thinkin' about it now."

"I hope so. Do you hear anything?"

"Just the regular squirrels and birds and foxes—"

"Is that a fox or a dog?"

Jasmine stopped and listened carefully. "It be a fox," she said.

Before they slept that night, they dried their clothes out by the fire.

Malinda ran her fingers through her hair in an attempt to get out the tangles. "I'll plait it," she said and asked Jasmine to part her hair in the middle for two braids.

"You does that real good." Jasmine watched with interest.

Malinda chuckled. "I should. About ten of papa's cows have plaited tails because of me."

"How come?"

"I learned how on them, that's how come. I bet I put fifteen tiny plaits in every cow's tail. . . . Those tiny things got so tangled up, most of them are still plaited together after four years."

Jasmine's eyes sparkled. "You has enough practice on them cows to do this good?"

"No. Mama let me braid hers, too—but only if I'd do them big." Malinda tied the braid ends of her hair into a knot. "Mama wouldn't redo her braids either—even when I got them crooked."

"Plaited cow's tails! I has heard everything now!"

When Malinda had finished, Jasmine got her to write out each letter of the alphabet on the cave floor.

"I'll write them out wherever you like until you can carry them around in your memory."

"Okay. Now we gets a little sleep before we poles on that river tonight."

It was almost dawn, however, when a congregation of mockingbirds awoke them. The crisp coolness, in contrast to yesterday's warmth, urged them onto the raft rather than waiting through another day for darkness. When they neared the raft, Jasmine held Malinda back.

"Stay here. Something's on them logs."

"What is it?"

They both stared at the raft.

"It's a bundle, Jasmine. It isn't ours."

"I knows."

They hid behind a bush and waited. When several minutes had passed and nothing happened, they ventured a little nearer the water's edge.

"Maybe it float up there while we was sleepin'."

A voice sounded behind them. "It didn't float up. I put it there."

Both girls jerked around. Malinda planted herself protectively in front of Jasmine. *Help me do the right thing,* she prayed, and hoped God was listening.

"Yes, ma'am. What do you want?" Malinda stammered as her gaze searched the tall plump woman, perhaps her own mother's age, who loomed in front of her. Her heart jumped like leap frogs as she waited for an answer.

"I sho am curious. What're you girls doin'?" The stranger's voice was firm.

This woman had to believe her. "We're . . . just on an adventure. Papa said I could explore this side of the river as long as I had Jasmine along."

"And where's your pa?"

"He's trappin' downriver a ways. We'll meet up with him in a couple of hours."

The woman smoothed out her muslin dress and her bright clean apron. *I didn't convince her,* Malinda thought. *And now I'm tongue-tied.*

"Honey, you don't have any cause to be afraid of me."

Malinda turned toward Jasmine for help.

The black girl poked her head around Malinda. "Mistis want to know how come the bundle down there?" She nodded toward the raft.

The woman folded her arms across her chest. "It's good strappin' vittles. Now I don't know where you two come from or where you're goin', but I do know skin and bones when I see them. You need all the vittles I put in there and then some. So eat them up. And I put in some good liniment for your foot." She nodded to Jasmine.

"You saw us yesterday?"

The woman smiled broadly. "One of my young'uns strayed away from home and found you first. He fetched his pa, and his pa fetched me. We was afraid we would scare you off, but I knew you had to have some vittles. You sure you girls ain't lost?"

"No—no, ma'am. We know the Tombigbee."

"My man and me can help you get found if you're lost."

Malinda hesitated.

Jasmine popped out again. "Thanky, ma'am, but massa expect us back by noontime."

"I sho am curious." The woman shook her head slowly. "And you haven't satisfied my curiousness a bit."

"We don't understand, ma'am."

"I guess we can't keep you here if you're bound to leave, but I sho would hate to know we hadn't done our duty." She pushed back a strand of dark hair from her face. "If your pa is nearby, you tell him to feed you better, you hear? And if he isn't nearby, I just hope those vittles last you till you get home."

Malinda walked over and took the woman's rough hands in hers. "Thank you! You're kind.

. . . You're very kind."

"Git! Git!" Jasmine shouted and limped through the trees toward the river. "Thievin' old possum! Git!"

"You get, too," the woman said gently to Malinda. "We've fed that possum so long he ain't scared of nothin' when food's around."

"Yes, ma'am."

The woman still held Malinda's hands. "You take care. For my peace of mind, I got to believe you know where you're goin'."

"We do—we promise. Goodbye." Malinda sprinted after Jasmine who had not succeeded in chasing the possum off their raft. He crouched on a corner as if he would tumble off into the water any minute and watched them with beady eyes. Jasmine poked at him with one of the poles they had fashioned to push the raft, but he clung to the corner log by his long hairless tail and played dead until Jasmine turned her back. Malinda poked him with her pole.

Jasmine inspected the bundle. "We caught him before he got inside."

"It looks like he caught us, too. He isn't budgin'."

"Let's be a-pushin' off then. We can get rid of him later."

With their poles they moved the raft out of the bayou toward the open river, and waved at the woman until they rounded the bend.

"We sho didn't do so well yesterday after all. Three people were watchin' us." Malinda shivered.

Jasmine glanced at the food. "I sho is glad this time."

"I smell ham. I guess maybe we found one of those angels from heaven."

"Huh! I take her any day to a angel I ain't never seen."

The possum curled his tail around a log for support and fixed his eyeballs on the bundle as Jasmine began examining its contents. Malinda poled close to the banks heading downstream.

"I told you! Ham, Malindy, and corn bread and sweet taters and milk. Two jars of milk! We is rich!"

"Amen! With a possum thrown in."

Jasmine handed Malinda a piece of meat and then threw a scrap to the possum. She was humming a soft tune.

Oh go and tell it on de mountain,
   Jesus done bless my soul
Oh go and tell it in de valley,
   Jesus done bless my soul.

TRAVLER

THE FIRST TIME they hid out of sight from a boat, Malinda dressed Jasmine's foot with the liniment. The possum nudged at the pottery bowl and pot covering their remaining food with his long snout. They had decided it would be wise to stretch out their "manna from the heavens," as Jasmine called it, and not gorge themselves all in one day.

Jasmine hummed as they pushed downriver, sometimes singing softly, but always the same song.

Don't be weary, traveler,
　Come along home, come home.

Don't be weary, traveler,
　Come along home, come home.

"I never heard you sing before yesterday,"
Malinda said.

"Ain't nobody around. Besides, I's happy."

It *was* good to be on the river again, and
even the woods lining the shore did not look as
dark and sinister as they had earlier from
their canoe. Neither the day's chill nor the
frequent times they must take cover from
river traffic dampened their spirits.

By the end of the day Malinda, at Jasmine's
insistence, had carved all the letters of the
alphabet on the logs of the raft with Jasmine's
knife. The possum evidently thought she was
trying to play with him every time she squat-
ted to work on the letters. He pushed his snout
towards her or scratched at her with a foot.
When she poked at him, he scurried back to
his favorite corner and played dead.

Jasmine traced each letter with a finger
when Malinda finished it. "How you make
Jeb?"

Malinda sounded it out slowly. "I think it's
J-E-B."

"This be *J* for Jeb." Jasmine pointed with
confidence to the right letter.

"For Jasmine, too."

The other girl looked startled. "Where be *E*?"

Jasmine traced each letter with her finger once again. Then she stood and resumed her poling but was soon outlining the three letters, *J-E-B*, with her big toe. "I got it now, Malindy."

Malinda was carving *Z*. "Where *is* Jeb?" she asked.

Jasmine frowned but said nothing.

"Do you really know?"

"I knows. But sometimes I forgets. Reckon these letters will help me remember if I sees it writ out?"

"Jasmine, is there really a Jeb?"

"I says so. Ain't that enough?"

Malinda gazed at Jasmine's big black eyes, her deep brown cheeks, her black bonnet of curls—all etched in Malinda's memory as permanently as the alphabet on their raft.

"Yes, Jasmine, that's enough."

Jasmine sighed heavily. "He passes word to me that all I gotta do in Mobile is get on most any boat, and it be takin' me north."

"What about the ones that go to New Orleans?"

"That ain't the sound of the place I's goin'."

Malinda fell silent. For days—weeks—she had pondered Jasmine's escape plan, but now she didn't want to think about it anymore. In fact, it made her feel ill to consider their separation. She stared at her now, absorbed as she was in tracing her toe over *B,* and felt suddenly chilled.

"Jasmine, I didn't like playin' mistress this mornin'."

Jasmine straightened, stared intently downriver, and then looked at her. "Me neither. It ain't us."

"Of course, I know you nursed me back to life for me to help you that way, and I don't want to quit helpin' you. That's not it at all."

"You helps in lots of ways. But I had other reasons for gettin' you over the fever."

"You did?" Malinda brightened. "Like what?"

"Well, has you got to ask? I reckon the Lord sorta use me, as the preacher say, 'cause you be dead if I not find you."

"It sounds like you think God is takin' care of us," she said.

"Ain't I been singin' Jesus done bless my soul?"

Malinda nodded.

"I don't know much about this Jesus," Jasmine continued. "Most the time the preacher talk about how us slaves got to do what massa tell us. But sometimes a black preacher come around, and he be some preacher! Massa let us go down in the fields to hear him."

Jasmine gave out a deep, satisfied chuckle. "Massa just not know how that preacher talk about a freedom-lovin' Jesus."

"Our preacher came about four times a year," Malinda said. "But not a night passed that mama and papa didn't read the Bible. And I can remember how Jesus said, 'I am with you always.'"

"See there!" Jasmine clapped her hands. "He knows I could make you well, so I figures that's one reason I find you in the woods."

"What's the other reason?"

"He knowed I needed you, I reckon."

Malinda took a deep breath. "Next time we run across anybody, we'll just be ourselves —me and you."

"There ain't gonna be no next time. It be easier for us this way, all by ourselves."

Malinda shivered. "It's gettin' cold."

"You looks pale, Malindy. You better not get sick when we got good food for the first time."

Malinda shook her head, saying she felt fine when she really didn't—not as long as she was wondering what would happen to the two of them if they ever got to Mobile.

Soon after they started out on the river the next morning, Jasmine announced they were naming the possum Travler.

"For your song," Malinda said.

"Uh-huh. But if we ever gets on hard times, he gonna travel right into our soup."

As if they had not been through some hard times. The ham and sweet taters and corn bread—and the quiet Tombigbee—were making them forget. Malinda gazed deep into the forest as they glided past. It looked protective as if beckoning them to safety if the river turned against them. Did she no longer feel revulsion for the wilderness trail? She wanted to sing out that they had made the right decision to return to the river, but instead she joined Jasmine in her low song—just above a whisper.

Keep a-goin', traveler,
    Come along home, come home.
Keep a-singin' all the way,
    Come along home, come home.

Just where to go I did not know,
    Come along home, come home.
A travelin' long and a travelin' slow,
    Come along home, come home.

That night they could not sleep in the freezing wind that made their fire sputter and sucked all its warmth away. They built it as high as they dared and stationed themselves between it and the wind, but still they ached with cold. After two dreadful hours they returned to the raft, pushing their poles vigorously in the moonlight to chase away the cold.

Intent upon their task, a steamboat's shrill whistle from downriver startled and frightened them. They hunted for overhanging limbs of evergreens but, seeing none, had to ground the raft and hide behind tree trunks. The long wait for the boat to pass was agony. They ate a piece of meat and concentrated on savoring the strong, rich flavor of each bite, chewing slowly in a vain attempt to freeze out of their minds all sensations other than taste.

Once the boat was safely past, its lights unable to pick them out, they moved swiftly on the Tombigbee River as if frozen in position on the raft, moving silently—no song on their lips.

Daylight brought no relief, for the sun could not penetrate the heavy clouds. They stayed on the river fighting time and weather, but at last they were forced to stop from exhaustion. They jumped up and down and ran back and forth as they gathered brush for a fire, continuing to pile on limbs after the flames had a good start. They turned first one side and then the other to the heat, and only when they felt completely comfortable did they settle down to eat from their diminishing bundle and take turns napping.

Seated with her arms around her knees, Malinda moved her back dangerously close to the fire as she kept vigil. If only the sun would break through the clouds . . . But Jasmine wasn't asleep after all; she was mumbling although her eyes were closed.

"I's been a-wonderin', Malindy."

"What are you wonderin'?"

"About us—I mean, if we don't freeze and gets there, what is we gonna do in Mobile?"

Jasmine's question echoed her own.

"Is you got brothers and sisters?"

"No. Have you?"

"No. I has always wondered what it like to have a sister—and ma and pa."

Malinda twisted around slowly, gazing through the warm flames at Jasmine curled up on the other side. She lay so still, her eyes closed, that she could have dozed off to sleep. A damp log sizzled in the heat, and two redbirds high in a pine drowned out the mockingbirds with their song.

Her face cradled in her arms, Jasmine finally spoke again, her words muffled against her sleeve. "If I stays in Mobile, do you reckon massa come lookin' for me that far away?"

What was she saying? That she would not head north? But she had just said yesterday—or was it the day before—that nothing would stop her from finding Jeb.

"I don't know. I saw a newspaper on the steamboat askin' for information about runawayers," Malinda said gently, miserable as she contemplated the end of their journey.

Suddenly Jasmine sat up and stared back at her through the flames. "But what about out West? Reckon massa find me there?"

Again Malinda shook her head. "I don't know. I thought you were goin' north to Jeb."

"I guess so. But first I got to know if you and your pa—well, is you ever comin' north?"

"I don't know that either, Jasmine. . . . Would you maybe stay in Mobile?" She held her breath for the answer.

Jasmine smiled. "Sho I would. Me and you, well—"

"We been through some hard times together. But I have to know, Jasmine, if we can stay just me and you when we get there."

"I reckon so. You sho don't act like a mistis—"

"I couldn't."

"I knows. And I be free, too. So that just leaves me and you 'cause I sho ain't gonna act like no slave. Your Aunt Eliza gonna like me, too. . . . You think our hard times is over, Malindy?"

Malinda hesitated a long time before answering. "I hope so, Jasmine."

She knew neither of them could yet predict their future.

COME ALONG HOME

THEY WERE ALMOST ready to stop for two or three hours of sleep, having abandoned their fire early in the afternoon and pushed out into the cold and continued long into the night.

"Soon's we get by this swampy place, let's stop. I sho could stand it," Jasmine said.

"And we'll have some greens and corn bread with the potlicker," Malinda said, beginning the fantasy in which they often indulged.

"And black-eyed peas and ham and chicken and blackberry pie."

"And buttermilk and hot sweet taters—"

"Aw, go on! Who wants them when we has cold ones?"

They began to laugh.

"I feels it, Malindy. Good things a-comin'. Me and you is gonna make it home, wherever home is, and I got a feelin' it be Mobile."

Malinda's spirits lifted.

Soon they were past the swamp and hunting for a good place to stop. High banks or stagnant swampland lined the river's edge. Finally they pulled the raft in between gum and cypress trees until it was out of the water and then gathered wood for a fire. Travler sat on the raft with their food. It seemed to take Jasmine forever to get sparks from the flint she was striking against the hatchet. When at last the long brown pine needles they had gathered were burning, it was a beautiful sight. They lit the dry leaves and needles under the heavier wood and blew on the tiny flames until the fire caught up.

Her teeth aching, Malinda rubbed her arms and legs until they hurt, trying to restore her circulation, and then she loped back to the raft for their food. In addition to a few berries, they would have half of a sweet potato and a hunk of ham, which would leave enough for one more day's meager feast.

The rest of the night was unbearably long, interspersed by feeding the fire, a little sleeping, and listening to wolves in the distance.

Once Jasmine asked, "Did your ma teach you how to make a dress like that?"

"No, she taught me how to crochet, and I've made a right pretty sampler—"

"Good! You teach me to read, and I teach you to sew—lace and ruffles and ribbons, too. You can sho stand a heap of cleanin' up."

"Your baggy trousers—"

"Yep, we gonna get rid of them, too."

"We're still on the Tombigbee. Let's not think about Mobile yet."

"That be okay with me, but sometimes my mind runs on in spite of myself."

With the first streak of dawn, they were back on the raft, a light breeze blowing from the south giving them hope for a warmer day. When the sun came up over the horizon, they wanted to shout but dared not.

They had not been traveling long before Malinda voiced her feelings. "I can't put my finger on it, but somethin's different down here, Jasmine. It feels like—well, like we're the only humans for a thousand miles."

"Somethin's different all right. What is them sticky things?"

"Palmettos."

"And there be a bobwhite."

Then they saw a pomegranate tree and headed for shore. As they picked as many as they could reach, they saw deer fleetingly in the forest.

"How beautiful!"

"It be a wonder nobody ain't huntin' them."

"These dense forests haven't been touched. We're alone in these parts except for the animals and birds—and it's creepy."

"I don't believes you this time, Malindy. Somebody is got to be in them woods somewheres."

Back on the raft, they each tore the skin off a large round pomegranate and nibbled on the sweet red seeds, spitting the bitter cores into the water once the sweetness was gone. At home pomegranate juice, cooled in spring water, had been a favorite treat.

"Look at the canebrakes ahead! They're as big as all out yonder!"

"We's gonna do without them!" Jasmine glanced at her foot, which was healing better now that she was not walking on it and was regularly using the liniment the woman had given her.

"This time we just gonna pole right by them," she said.

They had seen many patches of the bamboolike reeds growing three or four feet high in the swamps and bayous, but none covered such a wide area as these. Here the canebrake extended out from the shore so far that they were soon a good distance from the forest.

"We is way out here for the Lord and everybody to see."

"The river's widening, too. Look out there!" Malinda pointed ahead.

"That ain't no river. It be a ocean. What is we gonna do?"

"We'll keep the raft close to the canebrakes just as we've stayed close to the shoreline. Maybe we're gettin' near Mobile and the 'Bigbee is runnin' into the bay."

"What bay?"

Malinda told her what she knew about Mobile Bay. Ahead the water seemed to flow into a huge hole in the sky. It was difficult to see any shore on either side. How dreadful to be moving so far out to go around the canebrakes. But only small ripples pushed by a gentle wind marred the smooth surface. Travler slept. A turkey vulture sat in a leafless tree far ahead viewing the countryside.

They saw quail and doves in the cane. "If we just had papa's shotgun, we could grow fat on our eatin'."

"Uh-huh, and have the whole countryside out lookin' for who blowed off that gun."

Malinda gazed far into the distance where water and sky blended so well that she could not tell where one ended and the other began.

As they poled along sometimes they talked;

sometimes they didn't. Once Jasmine said, "I still likes this better than a-slavin' at the big house."

"You sure are spunky."

"I reckon you is, too."

Malinda looked toward the woods far away. "No, I'm not. I've been scared to death lots of times." It seemed easy to admit it to Jasmine now. She relaxed and watched the other girl's strong arms pole the raft along with the current.

"You not act like it, most of the time anyways."

"It's funny, Jasmine. I don't feel as scared anymore, but the night mama died—"

"Anybody be scared then."

"But papa was deep in the woods. Mama got worse, and I had to go find him, Jasmine. And I got lost—and—"

Malinda shivered. She couldn't tell her about the other runawayer.

Jasmine stopped poling to listen.

"And when . . . when I found him we rushed back to mama, but it was too late. He did everything he knew to do, Jasmine, while I just stood by and watched. But I was so afraid."

"Sho you was."

"Are you ever afraid?"

"Sho is. When I runned away, I thought

every noise in the woods was them devil slavers."

"How could you try again after bein' caught
the first time?"

"Jeb! I just think about Jeb, Malindy, and
the hate I feel for massa get me started again."

"Do you think Jeb knows you're on the
way?"

Jasmine brooded over the matter. "I believes so, Malindy," she whispered.

After a long silence, Jasmine added, "When
the steamboat exploded, I runned so fast a
chicken could have sat on my shirttail. Then I
hears somebody else crashin' through the
woods, and I knowed them slavers find me
again. Scared! Malindy, I ain't never been so
scared."

"What happened?"

"It was you! I find you at daylight, and I
praise God and promise him to make you well.
I sho is glad he help me do it!"

"I am, too."

"The noises in the woods don't scare me,
Malindy, when I be with you. So don't you
think Jeb want me to stay with you?"

"He loves you, Jasmine. I'm sure he wants
you with him."

Jasmine frowned, "I don't think so. You be a
friend. . . . Why, Malindy, you ain't even white
anymore."

"I know! Weather worn and dirty—that's what I am."

"That not be what I mean."

Excitement welled inside Malinda. If Jasmine wanted to, surely they could stay together in Mobile. Aunt Eliza would take her in, too, until papa came for them. They could both go to school; they could study together; they could play and shout and sing out loud, unafraid. Malinda pushed hard with her pole, eager to come to the end of their journey since they would not have to separate.

"All this big water is makin' waves." The surging river slashed against the raft as Malinda checked the vines that held the logs secure in their notches. "I wish they would quit."

"They maybe ain't gonna quit. Look, Malindy!"

Dark clouds were rolling in far to the south, although the sun was still shining where the girls were. Malinda checked the shoreline. As far as she could see, several hundred feet of gigantic cane separated them from the firm ground where the woods began. Suddenly the river current swirled them swiftly away, their poles as helpless as thin reeds.

"Watch out!" Malinda yelled.

The raft slammed into a boulder partially exposed above the water. They pushed away from it with their poles only to find that the impact had severed their logs from the notches enough that the river current ripped away the vines, tugged at the logs, and sent them peeling off in different directions.

"Grab a log! Grab a log!" Malinda was yelling almost before she surfaced after their plunge. Jasmine had already latched on to one.

"I's kickin', Malindy!"

Malinda snatched at a log whirling past, moving swiftly with the current. Jasmine stayed afloat on hers, just as she had behind the raft that warm day she had learned to swim. But now the river was as cold as spring water.

"Kick and try to work toward the cane!" Malinda yelled. Her wet skirt weighed her down, but the current was too strong for them to control their direction. Ahead the cane thicket extended farther out into the river, and they were headed straight for it.

"Watch for rocks!" Jasmine called. Seeing several jutting out of the water ahead, Malinda let go of her log and swam to them. Looking back to see that Jasmine was making it, she jumped from one rock to another until she was once again in the tall reed grass. When Jasmine joined her, they heard a rustling beneath them and jumped with fright back onto a slippery rock in the river. A soaked possum peered at them from the bamboo cane.

"That stupid possum is gonna be the ruin of us yet!" Malinda grabbed him by the neck and set him on her shoulder. "Now stay there!"

The logs from their raft swirled out again toward mid-river. Jasmine struggled to find a couple of medium-sized rocks.

"Just in case we needs them," she said as she heaved up one and then relinquished it for two smaller ones.

Malinda had used so much of her shirt for Jasmine's foot bandages that only the shoulders and sleeves remained, which she used as a belt to hold up her loose dress. She patted her round white pebble, knotted up in the end of one sleeve, and noted with satisfaction that it was not lost. Jasmine still carried the small Tombigbee pebbles in one pants pocket.

A boat horn sounded low and mournful in the quiet. Smoke rose against the distant sky.

"Malindy . . ." Jasmine sounded hesitant. "Did you hear a shotgun when that boat horn blew?"

Malinda shook her head. "Why?"

"I thinks I did."

"If there was one shot, I bet there would be others. I think it was just the horn."

"I don't know."

They walked side by side, each stepping carefully on the undergrowth and vines in an attempt to miss the prickles.

"It's impossible to get through this cane-brake," Malinda said.

"You just put one foot in front of the other and forget everything else."

Black birds were flying overhead, and geese skied across the water to land beyond the swirling current where the raft had broken up. Each step was a struggle. Malinda stopped so that she could measure with her eye how far it was to land and, watching the wild fowl, she suddenly felt hungry.

"Here! I got a piece of pomegranate." Jasmine had a difficult time getting it out of her soaked pants; but when she did, they divided it between them. They gave the peelings to Travler who still rode Malinda's shoulder.

"Jasmine, look how far we've come from the river. No way at all."

"We ain't looking behind us, Malindy. We keeps our eyes just on them woods ahead and what be under our feet."

They were more than halfway through the canebrake when something came crashing in their direction from their right.

"Run!" Jasmine yelled.

"I can't."

"You gotta!"

They didn't wait to see what it was. They tried to run. They swung at the reeds blocking their way and had no time to pick and choose where they were stepping. Malinda's foot caught in a clump of vines. She fell. At the same time she heard a wild squeal behind her.

"Run, Jasmine! Keep on runnin'!"

Through the cane rushed a huge, sandy-colored wild boar, its two long swordlike tusks and its two short stumpy ones, headed straight at her.

A rock zinged over her head from Jasmine's hand, and the boar squealed again. Jasmine, still clinging to her one remaining rock, yanked Malinda up as she struggled to rise. They were running, but what was the use? She knew how fast a boar could run. Papa had killed one once, but not before it had chased down a horse and cut it to shreds.

Malinda glanced back as she ran. The white tusks were gaining on them. Ears the size of papa's hands and red evil eyes, partly covered with shaggy hair, bore down on them. The canebrake was not opening up to let them through.

PROPER PAPERS

SO IT WAS ALL going to end right here in the canebrake. The past weeks—their struggles and fevers and fears and, yes, their songs and laughter—appeared before her like a mirage. The hovering forest ahead was the promised land. If only one of those trees were out here so they could scale it in a flash and be free of this monster.

She kept hearing Jasmine's voice as if coming from the far end of a rain barrel. . . . "Me and you's gonna make it home, Malindy. . . . We keep our eyes just on them woods ahead. Me and you and the Lord, Malindy. . . ."

Through the cane rushed a huge, sandy-colored boar.

Throwing caution aside, she screamed for help, knowing full well there was no one to assist them in this desolate countryside. Jasmine's last rock flew over her head. It landed far to their right. The boar squealed. Then Jasmine dug the Tombigbee pebbles out of her pocket. She threw them in the same direction as the other rock. The boar veered off course and began butting the ground around the stones in fury.

The momentary relief gave Malinda a new spurt of energy.

"Run, Malindy!"

The boar was silent. The rocks had diverted him, but Malinda knew it would not be for long. She and Jasmine lunged forward toward the forest. The cane thicket clawed at them. With a violent squeal the boar plunged toward them again, and again Malinda screamed for help. She must get control of herself and use anything at her disposal to try to save them.

Anything! The heavy weight on her shoulder. She raised her hand to grab him by the tail and sling him into the canebrake to divert the boar when Travler made a flying leap and landed on the boar's bristled back. His cavernous mouth white with foam, the boar chased himself around and around trying to slash the possum riding him. The girls plunged ahead as fast as they could in the canebrake, but the possum never lost his balance until the boar rolled over on his back, his stubby legs in the air. Travler leaped off before he was crushed and dashed into the undergrowth. But in no time the swifter animal overcame him and slashed him to pieces with his long tusks.

Tears were streaming down the girls' cheeks as they ran. Now they had nothing: no raft or food or hatchet, or possum, or much strength or time. . . .

Once the boar had finished off Travler, he flew toward Jasmine and Malinda. Malinda kept her eyes on the trees. They were nearer, much nearer now—although she could hear the boar gaining on them. When Jasmine tripped and Malinda stopped to help her, they could see the white tusks flashing through the cane. *It's just me and you and the Lord, Jasmine,* she thought.

A single shot fired out from the trees. The sound pierced Malinda's consciousness, but she kept running. The boar had squealed wildly but was still crashing toward them. In another minute, however, all was silent. She turned her head long enough to see the boar's large body slumped in the canebrake, blood running down between its evil red eyes. Then she rushed toward firm ground as if still pursued. Three more steps would bring them out of the canebrake . . . now two . . . now one.

They ran well in under the pines before they collapsed on the soft brown carpet of needles, crying hysterically and hugging each other. Now their bleeding feet began to ache. With a tremor on their lips, they smiled at each other.

"Me and you and the Lord, we done made it, Malindy!" Jasmine gasped slowly.

Malinda looked up through the beautiful green pines to the clouding sky in thanksgiving. Perched high on a limb near the edge of the forest where the canebrake began sat a young man holding a gun. He was staring at them and smiled when he saw they had discovered him. He slid down the firm straight trunk of the pine and stood hesitantly where he landed.

"Oh, thank you!"

"Thank you!"

"Thank God!" he replied.

"The Lord sent you!"

"We's on speaking terms now and then," the stranger said in a deep rich voice. "But right now I gotta get you home so's Missy can take care of you."

"Where be home?" Jasmine demanded.

"I got a shack in these woods."

Jasmine brushed a tear off Malinda's cheek with a grubby thumb and gave her a brilliant smile. "See, Malindy, there was another human in a thousand miles—"

"Thank God!"

The man was helping them up. "I can't carry you both, but I ain't leavin' one of you here alone, so you both just lean on me and let my arms support you best they can. Let me carry your weight instead of your feet doing it."

"Wait!" Jasmine demanded again. "Who be at your shack?"

"Missy, she be my woman, and a couple of chilluns."

"Where the massa and mistis?"

"Ain't got none. I's free."

"You dead sure?"

The man smiled. "I's dead sure."

Jasmine was satisfied. "I lean on you then."

By nighttime—with torn feet bandaged and their bodies and heads scrubbed in a washtub and a supper of dove and peas and corn bread in their stomachs—Jasmine and Malinda rested by the fire in Missy's and William's cabin. The children were sound asleep in a big bed in the corner. The girls related their story, although Malinda could tell by her eyes that Jasmine was still suspicious. She kept asking them how long they had lived there, how they had come by their freedom, and could she see what a freedom paper looked like?

Once she saw it, she exclaimed, "Malindy, I still got the letters you taught me. They's written here, and I remember them."

Missy looked puzzled so they told all about their raft, and Jasmine repeated the alphabet without any prompting; then reported she could count, too. But when she rummaged in her pants for the piece of wood with a notch for each day, she discovered her secret pouch containing the stick and the piece of flint. Her knife was gone.

"What is I gonna do?" she wailed.

Missy smiled. "We take care of you."

"But me and Malindy got to go—" she stopped and looked cautiously at Malinda.

"We got to go home, wherever our home is," Malinda added, repeating the exact words Jasmine had stated so confidently—was it only yesterday?

"We have to get *you* to Mobile," William said to Malinda.

"How come?"

"Because your pa is turnin' the world upside down for you."

"What do you mean?" Malinda's heart pounded in anticipation.

"We been keepin' up with your pa in the papers," Missy said gently. And then it was their turn to relate how her papa had heard about the steamboat explosion some five days after it had occurred. When Malinda was un-accounted for, he went to his sister's in Mobile where he contacted the steamboat offices for traces of her. Now, he was still searching up and down the river.

"He say you learn from him how to survive like a Injun," William added admiringly. "And since you wasn't one of them accounted for among the livin' or the dead, he say you got to be alive somewheres. And hallelujah! You sho is!"

"I wouldn't be, though, if it weren't for Jasmine findin' me and nursin' me well."

"I's not be here to tell about it, neither, if Malindy not save me from drownin'."

"How you happen to come on Malindy so deep in the woods?" Missy wanted to know.

Jasmine's large eyes flicked once toward Malinda. If any telling was to be done, it was up to her; Malinda wasn't giving her secret away under any circumstances. Jasmine lowered her gaze to where her hands lay in her lap.

"I's a runawayer."

"I thought so," William said matter-of-factly. "You ain't got no pass, so you can't go to Mobile."

Jasmine was indignant. "I's with Malindy!"

"We're together. Nobody gonna separate us!" Malinda cried.

Missy leaned over and put an arm around Jasmine's shoulders. "Honey, Malindy can't help you. It be spread all over the countryside that she be travelin' alone on that boat. Ain't no way for her to pretend to be your mistis."

"I'm not her mistis. We're friends."

"Then we can go into town different ways—alone," Jasmine said.

"No!" William's voice was sharp. "You'd be picked up and sold right off the auction block."

"What does you mean?"

"Listen!" William put his face in his strong hands for a brief moment before he continued. "If you is alone somebody gonna demand your pass, and if it ain't real official—where you going and what for, when you left, when you return, and a unsuspicious signature of your massa—you gets took to the auction block."

"Even free blacks with proper papers has sometimes been picked up and sold," Missy added.

"It don't happen everywhere, but it do in Mobile."

"You said you're a shepherd and sell cattle and vegetables in Mobile," Malinda said. "How do *you* get around?"

"Me and a white farmer friend over yonder goes together."

"Do he have slaves?" Jasmine demanded.

"No."

"Does you have to pretend he's your massa?"

"No. Sometimes I has to show my freedom papers, but he always be there to help me. We never gets away from each other very far."

"Then I'll stay here, and you can go fetch my papa," Malinda said to William. She couldn't leave Jasmine; no one had better ask her to leave Jasmine.

William and Missy looked at each other for a long still moment. She rose and went over and stood behind his chair next to the fire, a hand on his shoulder. He put his hand up and patted hers as he spoke.

"Malindy, we can help you get to Mobile. And Jasmine, we can help you get away safe from your massa. But we can't bring nobody in here to us."

"Why not?" Panic was rising in Malinda's chest.

"Because we got ourselves and others to protect."

"You is talkin' in riddles!" Jasmine retorted. "Explain yourself!"

"We is so far back in the woods nobody ever runned across us," Missy replied.

"And," William paused and squeezed Missy's hand, "we helps lots of our people—just like we can help you, Jasmine—and we wants to keep on with it."

Malinda moved over close to Jasmine. William's message had finally gotten through to her. He had some way to help people like Jasmine escape to freedom, and he was not going to bring the world to his doorstep. "Is anybody suspicious of you?"

"Not at all." William spread his hands wide and smiled. "And I's gonna keep it that way—as I has for years now."

Malinda wiped unashamedly at a tear running down her cheek and salting her lips. "You sho don't give me and Jasmine much choice, do you?"

Missy poked at the coals and added another log to the fire. "They needs sleep, honey. Tomorrow will come soon enough. Then we can talk again."

"You's right," William responded. "Jasmine, I shift these chilluns over so's there be room for you on the bed. Malindy, you can have me and Missy's bed."

Jasmine drew herself up straight, her weight firm on her battered feet. "We is obliged for all you done for us, but we can't take you beds away, too. I reckon me and Malindy has bedded down by many a fire."

"Thank you just the same," Malinda added. "But we're gonna stay right here by this fire together."

FREE!

DESPITE ALL THE protection inside this home and all its cozy warmth, Malinda knew this was the cruelest fire she and Jasmine had shared. She knew it was to be their last.

How could it be otherwise? Now she had to face questions she had pushed harshly away. Separation sooner or later was inevitable. Even if they made the journey to Mobile successfully, how could they stay together for long unless they played maid and mistress? Soon the falseness and bitterness of that relationship would tear at their friendship, and they would be hating each other.

Tonight, in their first experience back in

civilization, even William had wanted to separate them—offering Malinda a whole bed to herself rather than offering it to them both. No, Malinda decided, despite the tears just behind her eyelids, there was no way they could be themselves—just Jasmine and Malinda—and stay together. If only they had lived in another time . . . another place . . .

She buried her face in the crook of her arm. Jasmine beside her on the floor moved, too. . . . Why must everyone she loved leave her? she wondered in desolate loneliness. And she could not go with Jasmine. If she did, she might never again find papa. She could see him in her memory standing on the shore, his hands in his pockets, while her own gripped the steamboat rail.

Malinda raised her head and gazed at the hot coals, the gray ashes, the black logs that sent out flames of red and purple and white and blue and green. When a hoot owl's lonely call sounded far away in the forest, Jasmine rolled over on her stomach and gazed into the fire, too. That was the way they spent the night—not needing to speak, lying side by side on the quilts and staring deep into the fire.

The next morning after the children were

outside playing, William explained how he could get Jasmine down the bay by boat, then transfer her to a ship on the Gulf of Mexico that would transport her to New York.

"What happens then? Will she have a home?"

"The cap'n on this ship will look out for her, and he has people in New York to help her as long as she needs them. She'll have a place to go immediately."

"How I know that boat not carry me back upriver to my massa?"

William was visibly stunned. "Jasmine, you can trust me."

"I ain't never seen you till yesterday, and you say I can trust you. *I* says I don't trust nobody! Once I got trusted right back to my massa's yard. This time I keeps to my own plan."

"You ain't got no massa!" William spoke with authority.

Jasmine stared at him speechless.

"You is free now. You ain't at nobody else's beck and call. I's just the instrument to see that you stays free, and you ain't free if you goes into Mobile."

"That be what you say. How does I know you tellin' me true? Besides, Malindy needs me through them woods."

It was Malinda's turn to stare, remembering again the time she had told Jasmine how she had been deathly afraid of the forest.

Had been . . . How beautiful it sounded! The small cabin could not contain her feelings. She escaped out the door and jumped down the two front steps, oblivious to her aching feet. As she landed on the ground she cried, "I'm free, too. I'm free! I'm not afraid of the woods anymore."

She had been freed and didn't even know it. Together she and Jasmine had beat back the wilderness and won.

Yesterday afternoon's clouds had spilled their rain, and now the resinous pines under which she walked scented the moist air. Cardinals were singing, and a distant crow cawed raucously. She could hardly keep up with her swift thoughts seesawing back and forth. She was not afraid of the reed grasses and canebrakes, and yet if William had not been there, they would have lost their lives in them yesterday. She had been terrified of the forest, but it had brought Jasmine and her together. Yesterday in their race against death, the trees had held out the possibility of life. . . . The wilderness had held tragedy for one runaway slave, but it had also protected another.

She gazed deep into the woods. The giant pines stood free of undergrowth across the land as far as she could see. The forest did not now torture her mind with the stench-filled fire and death of an unknown man. Instead it reminded her of the warm fires she and Jasmine had shared on their long journey, and of Jasmine's "G'night!" across the flames. Now she felt there was nothing in this wilderness she could not conquer if she tried.

I remember the very last words you told me, papa, she thought. *"You're going to come through on the other side." You had faith in me all the time.*

She was sitting on a log when Jasmine joined her. "How far is it to Mobile?" Malinda asked.

Jasmine flipped her head back toward the house. "He say not too far."

"I'm gonna walk all the way and see if my Aunt Eliza will keep me while I go to school."

"But your pa! He be here someplace looking for you. Ain't you goin' west with him?"

"Later maybe. But first I must grow up some and get more learnin'."

"I's comin' with you." Nobody wanted it more than Malinda. Her eyes ached as they met Jasmine's.

"I can't trust that William!" Jasmine said.

"How come? You trust me—at last. . . . And God, you trusted him all along."

"But I ain't laid eyes on William till yesterday."

"But Jasmine, he trusted *us*. He knows we aren't gonna tell anyone what he and Missy do, not even papa." She took a deep breath and blinked away the moisture in her eyes. "Besides, he killed that wild boar. And papa always said if somebody saves your life, that makes you blood kin. Can't you trust blood kin?"

Jasmine's eyes, getting bigger and rounder by the minute, clung to hers. They were both remembering the long fever days and the pebble tea and the storm waves and the overturned canoe.

Slowly Jasmine nodded her head, yes. Then she impulsively leaned over close to Malinda and spoke softly. "Love don't depend on time or place—I be rememberin' every word just like your ma said it."

"I'll be rememberin', too, Jasmine."

Jasmine smiled. "When I told you my name—well, it ain't really Jasmine."

"I know."

"You knowed all along?"

Malinda nodded.

"Well, I got to tell you my real name."

"You'll be Jasmine to me—always."

She leaned over and whispered her name in Malinda's ear, then drew back quickly with new understanding. "Oh, but I reckon I always be Jasmine to me, too. I give myself that name, and I likes it. It my *free* name."

"Will you keep it?"

"Sho I will."

"I'm glad, Jasmine, and I hope Jeb likes it, too."

Pain crossed Jasmine's face. "Jeb—he not make it, Malindy." She paused for a moment, looking through the trees. "He be killed when he runned away."

"But you said—"

"I knows. But I reckon I tells you what I wants to believe."

"Oh, Jasmine!"

"But don't you reckon maybe William can help me get where Jeb wanted me to go?"

Malinda nodded as she wiped away her tears. "I'm sure of it."

When William and Missy came out of the cabin, Malinda and Jasmine joined them at the steps.

"I wants to walk with Malindy through the woods when she leave," Jasmine said. "Then I do as you say."

"We is so glad you decided to accept our help," Missy said as she hugged Jasmine.

William added, "After we've given Malindy full directions and places where she can stop for help if she wants to—"

"And after I's fed her and wrapped up her feet and put some moccasins on them—"

"And I's gonna comb and plait her pretty brown hair—" Jasmine interrupted.

"Then we all walk with her as far as she needs us—but no more," William finished.

About a mile before the woods opened up into a clearing, William and Missy stopped and asked Malinda if she needed them any longer.

Trying hard to keep her voice even, Malinda said, "I can go the rest of the way by myself."

With their arms around each other, Missy and William watched her and waved as she kept going. Jasmine stayed by her side.

"Malindy, is you sure about these here woods? They can be mean."

"I'm sure, Jasmine. I'm not afraid anymore." The words tasted sweet as they left her lips.

Jasmine stopped, and Malinda turned to face her. They gazed at each other unable to take their eyes away.

Jasmine whispered, "We got good memories, ain't we?"

Malinda nodded.

"So we's rich."

Malinda nodded again.

She reached down in the pocket of her dress for her smooth white stone. It was wrapped in a piece of paper Missy had given her. Holding the warm pebble in her hand, she spread out the paper and gave it to Jasmine.

"Since your real name is Jasmine now, I wrote it out on this paper so you can spell it the way you learned to spell Jeb."

"How you know I wants to write my own name?"

Malinda gazed into Jasmine's black shimmering eyes. "I just felt it. Here!" Malinda took Jasmine's hand and put her pebble into it. Its crystals sparkled in the sunlight through the pines.

"What you doin'?"

"You gave this to me, Jasmine, a long time ago in some pebble tea. Now it's yours again."

"How come?"

"Because it's all I have."

Jasmine rubbed the stone with her fingers. "Maybe it be my star, too, Malindy."

"I hope so. It's daytime yet but, g'night, Jasmine."

"G'night, Malindy."

Malinda headed down the trail alone. She did not wave, but she knew Jasmine would be watching as long as she was in sight.

The Wonderful World of Adventure Books

CANAL BOY. Born in a log cabin on the Ohio frontier, James Garfield saw his youthful ambitions end in disappointments. Then he had what he called an "awakening" at a church meeting. With it came a new ambition: help others discover the purpose he now knew. He finished school, became headmaster—intended to spend his life teaching and preaching. But duty called him to be a general in the Civil War . . . to the Presidency—and an assassin's bullet. By Karin Clafford Farley. 20651—$1.95

THE PRISONERS' SWORD. Pity little Nathan Cowell, a Quaker boy in 17th-century England. When his father dies, authorities cite the Cowells' Quaker faith as an excuse to put them into jail and seize their farm. But through the efforts of an uncle, and William Penn—who founded the state of Pennsylvania—the Cowells are released. They set out for the New World, where Nathan is determined they shall have another farm. By Barbara Chamberlain. 16717—$1.75

HARVEST GOLD. This sequel to *Turkey Red* recalls more adventures from the "olden days" in the wheatlands of Kansas. Little Martha Friesen sees "God's way is best" as she realizes that moving away from her dearest friend enables her family to help establish a new church. She becomes a little missionary as she carries food to a bedfast Indian, and reads to him from the Bible. And how does he respond—with what favor does he repay her kindness? By Esther Vogt. 20800—$1.95

THE OTHER SIDE OF THE TELL. Adventures in a strange land that's much in the news these days—Israel. The characters: 12-year-old Jeff . . . his younger sister, Jennifer . . . their archaeologist parents . . . and Kerim, Jeff's Arab friend. The perils: a secret cave, and Arab guerrillas. A clue: watch for the ancient Christian symbol of the fish! Jeff grows up as he learns to rely on God. Great reading adventures for ages 10 and older! By Bettie Wilson Story. 95232—$1.50

Handy order form on last page

The Wonderful World of Adventure Books

AMBUSH! This book is 19 stories long—19 action-packed stories . . . set on the American frontier many years ago. Some of the stories are true—for instance, the story of Johnny Appleseed, who wandered the frontier, planting little seeds that grew into trees whose fruit delighted pioneer children. Also true—the story of a 13-year-old boy who led his six brothers and sisters on to Oregon after their parents died on the trail. Recommended for children 7-10.   08748—$1.95

GROWING-UP SUMMER. Mark is smaller than the other boys, but always trying to prove he is just as "grown up." His attempts often fail; he also seems to stumble in his Christian life. Is he trying too hard? Not waiting for the right signals? And how about Mark's family? They all yearn to move into a home of their own, yet they are beset by problems. It truly is a growing-up summer in every way for impatient Mark. A sequel to *City Kid Farmer* . . . by Jeanette Gilge.   96529—$1.50

THE CASTLE MYSTERY. Another thriller by Marjorie Zimmerman, author of *Treasure on Squaw Mountain.* Girls 10-14 will enjoy sharing the adventures of Gail Albright. Poor Gail—she couldn't have dreamed that a babysitting job for the summer could lead to such suspense and scares! Still, the big old house *is* like a castle—appropriate setting for the shrieks in the night . . . the blood spots on the rug . . . and the bony hand at the window. How will Gail survive!   15289—$1.95

Handy order form on last page

The Wonderful World of Pop-Up Books

Favorite Bible stories that "Pop Up" . . . full-color
scenes, often three dimensional . . . figures lift from
the scene when page is turned . . . other figures
move when tabs are pulled.

The Shepherds' Surprise. Child opens book, and shepherds raise up from the page . . . child pulls tab, and
angel appears in the clouds.　　　　　82362—$3.95

The Life of Moses. Hebrew slaves push a big stone,
chariot moves, bush burns, waters part . . . all as child
turns pages, pulls tabs, etc.　　　　　82370—$3.95

Jesus Lives! Gethsemane scene appears in 3D as book
opens . . . . Jesus appears in upper room when tab is
pulled . . . He ascends into clouds as page turns.

82388—$3.95

Noah's Animal Boat. Amazing action—Noah's saw
moves and sounds . . . animals and ark appear in 3-D
. . . ark tosses on the waves. More, too!　82396—$3.95

Handy order form
on last page

The Wonderful World of Teen Paperbacks

Never Miss A Sunset. Put yourself in Ellen's place: 75 years ago, on a backwoods farm in Wisconsin. Ellen is 13. She loves her family, but resents being second mother to her nine brothers and sisters. Then tragedy brings Ellen a guilt heavier than all her chores —a terrible burden that remains until winter warms into spring . . . to bring a time of new understanding for Ellen and her mother. · 86512—$1.95

City Kid Farmer. Won first prize in David C. Cook's 1975 children's book contest! You'll sympathize with Mark; he has to give up his friends when his folks move to the country. But worse, his aunt and uncle are just as "religious" as his mother. You'll see how Mark adjusts to rural life . . . and the chain of events that leads him to know Christ himself. 89474—$1.25

Pounding Hooves. More than an exciting horse story— it's the story of Lori's jealous struggle with her friend Darlene. Darlene probably will win the art contest. She'll win Ken, too—Darlene's so pretty! And Storm, the beautiful Arabian stallion—Darlene's father surely will buy him before Lori saves enough money. Rivals for so much . . . even with God's help, can Lori overcome her jealousy of Darlene? 89458—$1.75

Captured! Teenage adventure in wilderness America! Captured by Indians, Crist and Zack strike a bargain. The Indians want to learn more about the white man's ways, so the boys agree to teach the Indians—if they will spare their lives. But the boys would rather return home. Why, then, does Crist pass up a chance to escape? And Zack—why does he escape . . . then act so strangely when he finds the chief's son wounded, and helpless? · 87312—$1.50

Handy order form on last page

The Wonderful World of The Picture Bible

Easiest way imaginable to read the Bible—all the drama and excitement unfold vividly in black-and-white picture strips, easy-to-read dialogue, and captions.

All illustrations and statements authenticated by Bible scholars for biblical and cultured accuracy. Enjoy reading these 6 volumes:

OLD TESTAMENT

Creation: From "In the beginning" to the flight from Egypt

The Promised Land: Moses, Ten Commandments, Jericho

The Captivity: Divided kingdom falls . . . Israel is taken into captivity . . . prophecies of a coming Messiah

NEW TESTAMENT

Jesus: The Life of our Lord—His birth, ministry, first followers, crucifixion, and triumph over death

The Church: Angels announce Jesus will return . . . Pentecost . . . Stephen is stoned . . . Paul's conversion, missionary ministry, and death . . . the end of an era.

82701—All 6 books in slipcase. Set, $6.95

Handy order form on last page

The Wonderful World of Children's Books

THE SHAWL OF WAITING
Maybe you'd have done the same, if your grandmother had told you such a strange story. Anyway, after hearing her grandma's story, Emilie Coulter started to knit her own "shawl of waiting." Emilie knit, and knit—even if she didn't believe her grandma's story. But the more Emilie knit, the smaller the shawl became! Why couldn't she finish it?   89466—$1.25